PERILOUS OBSESSION

What Reviewers Say
About Carsen Taite's Work

Trial by Fire

"Ms. Taite brings something distinctive and special when she writes about law, something that tells her apart from the rest of the lesfic authors. I believe that's when she is at her best. Luckily for me, this is one of those books. ...This novel has the perfect balance between legal thriller and romance. Ms. Taite takes the reader to different legal proceedings and court action, all easy to understand for a layperson like me. It felt a bit like watching a courtroom movie."—*Lez Review Books*

Her Consigliere

"With this sexy lesbian romance take on the mobster genre, Taite brings savvy, confidence, and glamour to the forefront without leaning into violence. ...Taite's protagonists ooze competence and boldness, with strong female secondary characters. ...This is sure to please."—*Publishers Weekly*

"Such a great story! I was literally living for every moment in this. Both Royal and Siobhan were strong, powerful, authoritative women who I was absolutely captivated by. Their worlds and jobs were both edgy and exciting, providing that thrill of a little bit of danger along the way, especially when their emotions and affections for one another started to show. I adored them both and genuinely couldn't get enough of them. They were amazing!"—*LESBIreviewed*

Spirit of the Law

"I'm a big Taite fan, especially of her romantic intrigue books that are about some aspect of the law. She is one of the best writers out there when it comes to writing about courts and lawyers, so when you see a new book of hers in that category, you know you are in for a treat. And a treat is the perfect way to describe what reading Taite's books feel like, like eating a bowl of your favorite Ben and Jerry's ice cream."—*Lezreviewbooks*

Best Practice

"I had fun reading this story and watching the final law partner find her true love. If you like a delightful, romantic age-gap tale involving lawyers, you will like *Best Practice*. In fact, I believe you will like all three books in the Legal Affairs series." —*Rainbow Reflections*

Drawn

"This book held my attention from start to finish. I'm a huge Taite fan and I love it when she writes lesbian crime romance books. Because Taite knows so much about the law, it gives her books an authentic feel that I love. ...Ms. Taite builds the relationship between the main characters with a strong bond and excellent chemistry. Both characters are opposites in many ways but their attraction is undeniable and sizzling."—*LezReviewBooks.com*

Still Not Over You

"*Still Not Over You* is a wonderful second-chance romance anthology that makes you believe in love again. And you would certainly be missing out if you have not read *My Forever Girl* because it truly is everything."—*SymRoute*

Pursuit of Happiness

"This was a quick, fun and sexy read. ...It was enjoyable to read about a political landscape filled with out-and-proud LGBTQIA+ folks winning elections."—Katie Pierce, Librarian

"An out presidential candidate (Meredith Mitchell) who is not afraid to follow her heart during campaigning. That is truly utopia. A public defender (Stevie Palmer) who is leery about getting involved with the would-be president. The two women are very interesting characters. The author does an excellent job of keeping their jobs in focus while creating a wonderful romance around the campaign and intense media focus. ...Taite has written a book that draws you in. It had us hooked from the first paragraph to the last."—*Best Lesfic Reviews*

Love's Verdict

"Carsen Taite excels at writing legal thrillers with lesbian main characters using her experience as a criminal defense attorney." —*Lez Review Books*

Outside the Law

"[A] fabulous closing to the Lone Star Law Series. ...Tanner and Sydney's journey back to each other is sweet, sexy and sure to keep you entertained."—*Romantic Reader Blog*

"This is by far the best book of the series and Ms. Taite has saved the best for last. Each book features a romance and the main characters, Tanner Cohen and Sydney Braswell are well rounded, lovable and their chemistry is sizzling. ...The book found the perfect balance between romance and thriller with a surprising twist at the end. Very entertaining read. Overall, a very good end of this series. Recommended for both romance and thriller fans. 4.5 stars."—*Lez Review Books*

A More Perfect Union

"[*A More Perfect Union*] is a fabulously written tightly woven political/military intrigue with a large helping of romance. I enjoyed every minute and was on the edge of my seat the whole time. This one is a great read! Carsen Taite never disappoints!"
—*Romantic Reader Blog*

"Readers looking for a mix of intrigue and romance set against a political backdrop will want to pick up Taite's latest novel."
—*RT Book Review*

Sidebar

"As always a well written novel from Carsen Taite. The two main characters are well developed, likeable, and have sizzling chemistry."—Melina Bickard, Librarian, Waterloo Library (UK)

"Sidebar is a love story with a refreshing twist. It's a mystery and a bit of a thriller, with an ethical dilemma and some subterfuge thrown in for good measure. The combination gives us a fast-paced read, which includes courtroom and personal drama, an appealing love story, and a more than satisfying ending."
—*Lambda Literary Review*

Letter of the Law

"If you like romantic suspense novels, stories that involve the law, or anything to do with ranching, you're not going to want to miss this one."—*Lesbian Review*

Without Justice

"This is a great read, fast paced, interesting and takes a slightly different tack from the normal crime/courtroom drama. …I really enjoyed immersing myself in this rapid fire adventure. Suspend your disbelief, take the plunge, it's definitely worth the effort." —*Lesbian Reading Room*

"Carsen Taite tells a great story. She is consistent in giving her readers a good if not great legal drama with characters who are insightful, well thought out and have good chemistry. You know when you pick up one of her books you are getting your money's worth time and time again. Consistency with a great legal drama is all but guaranteed."—*Romantic Reader Blog*

Above the Law

"…readers who enjoyed the first installment will find this a worthy second act."—*Publishers Weekly*

Reasonable Doubt

"I liked everything. The story is perfectly paced and plotted, and the characters had me rooting for them. It has a damn good first kiss too."—*Lesbian Review*

Lay Down the Law

"This book is AMAZING!!! The setting, the scenery, the people, the plot, wow. …I loved Peyton's tough-on-the-outside, crime fighting, intensely protective of those who are hers, badass self."
—*Prism Book Alliance*

"I've enjoyed all of Carsen Taite's previous novels and this one was no different. The main characters were well-developed and intriguing, the supporting characters came across as very 'real' and the storyline was really gripping. The twists and turns had me so hooked I finished the book in one sitting."—Melina Bickard, Librarian, Waterloo Library (London)

Courtship

"Taite (*Switchblade*) keeps the stakes high as two beautiful and brilliant women fueled by professional ambitions face daunting emotional choices. …As backroom politics, secrets, betrayals, and threats race to be resolved without political damage to the president, the cat-and-mouse relationship game between Addison and Julia has the reader rooting for them. Taite prolongs the fever-pitch tension to the final pages. This pleasant read with intelligent heroines, snappy dialogue, and political suspense will satisfy Taite's devoted fans and new readers alike."—*Publishers Weekly*

Switchblade

"I enjoyed the book and it was a fun read—mystery, action, humour, and a bit of romance. Who could ask for more? If you've read and enjoyed Taite's legal novels, you'll like this. If you've read and enjoyed the two other books in this series, this one will definitely satisfy your Luca fix and I highly recommend picking it up. Highly recommended."—*C-Spot Reviews*

Battle Axe

"This second book is satisfying, substantial, and slick. Plus, it has heart and love coupled with Luca's array of weapons and a bad-ass verbal repertoire. ...I cannot imagine anyone not having a great time riding shotgun through all of Luca's escapades. I recommend hopping on Luca's band wagon and having a blast."—*Rainbow Book Reviews*

Beyond Innocence

"As you would expect, sparks and legal writs fly. What I liked about this book were the shades of grey (no, not the smutty Shades of Grey)—both in the relationship as well as the cases." —*C-spot Reviews*

Nothing but the Truth

"Taite has written an excellent courtroom drama with two interesting women leading the cast of characters. Taite herself is a practicing defense attorney, and her courtroom scenes are clearly based on real knowledge. This should be another winner for Taite."—*Lambda Literary*

It Should be a Crime—*Lammy Finalist*

"Taite, a criminal defense attorney herself, has given her readers a behind the scenes look at what goes on during the days before a trial. Her descriptions of lawyer/client talks, investigations, police procedures, etc. are fascinating. Taite keeps the action moving, her characters clear, and never allows her story to get bogged down in paperwork. *It Should Be a Crime* has a fast-moving plot and some extraordinarily hot sex."—*Just About Write*

By the Author

Truelesbianlove.com

It Should be a Crime

Do Not Disturb

Nothing but the Truth

The Best Defense

Beyond Innocence

Rush

Courtship

Reasonable Doubt

Without Justice

Sidebar

A More Perfect Union

Love's Verdict

Pursuit of Happiness

Leading the Witness

Drawn

Double Jeopardy (novella in Still Not Over You)

Spirit of the Law

Her Consigliere

Perilous Obsession

PERILOUS OBSESSION

by

Carsen Taite

2022

PERILOUS OBSESSION
© 2022 By Carsen Taite. All Rights Reserved.

ISBN 13: 978-1-63679-009-1

This Trade Paperback Original Is Published By
Bold Strokes Books, Inc.
P.O. Box 249
Valley Falls, NY 12185

First Edition: February 2022

Credits
Editor: Cindy Cresap
Production Design: Susan Ramundo
Cover Design By Tammy Seidick

Acknowledgments

I confess I'm a true crime junkie. Apparently, the many stories I encountered during my career as a criminal defense lawyer weren't enough of a fix because my wife, Lainey, and I will stay up into the wee hours watching Keith Morrison and friends digging deep to solve crimes and we're right there with them, following the evidence wherever it leads. I like to think my fascination with crime shows represents a craving for justice, and that's the inspiration for this book.

Thanks, as always, to Rad and Sandy and the entire crew at Bold Strokes Books for giving my stories a home at the best publishing house in the biz. Huge thanks to my smart, funny, and very patient editor, Cindy Cresap. Tammy, thank you for your thoughtful graphic design work on this and so many of my other covers.

The writing community has given me so many gifts, the most special of which is the friendships I've made during this journey. Big hugs to Georgia, Melissa, Kris, Elle, Ruth, and Ali. I don't get to see you all nearly enough, but when we get together, it's like coming home. Paula—thanks for being the best bestie a girl could have. You get me and I'm forever grateful for our friendship.

Thanks to Lainey for always believing in my dreams and sharing in my adventures. I couldn't live this dream without you, and I wouldn't want to. I can't wait to see what the future has in store for us.

And to you, dear reader, thank you for taking a chance on my work and coming back for more. Every time you purchase one of my stories, you give me the gift of allowing me to make a living doing what I love. Thanks for taking this journey with me.

Dedication

To Lainey and our present and future adventures.
I love building a life with you.

CHAPTER ONE

Calling units in the area, respond to a reported assault victim. White Rock Lake—8300 East Lawler. Ambulance on the way."

Macy eased off the accelerator and cranked the volume on her phone. It had become habit to tune in to the Dallas Police Department dispatch via the handy app she'd downloaded, but usually all that came across on her ride to work were a few sporadic bursts of calls about random vandalism and criminal trespass—nothing she'd be compelled to write about for the paper. She reached to turn the volume back down but stopped when the dispatcher's despondent tone announced: "Change that. Bus canceled. Jogger found a dead body."

Police responding to a call about a dead body wasn't all that unusual in a city the size of Dallas, but the location had caught Macy's attention, and her reporter brain kicked into high gear. She whipped her car into the exit lane and turned left onto Mockingbird Lane when she reached the light. While she impatiently waited for her turn to go, her phone buzzed with a text from her boss.

Where are you? Call me.

Jerry had been bugging her since last week for an update on the feature article that had consumed her time for the past few months, but she'd managed to put him off, promising she'd give him a status today, but today wasn't over yet. She almost picked up the phone and told him that, but decided against it, knowing then she'd have to answer his question about where she was headed.

Less than ten minutes later, she turned onto East Lawler, the road that led into the park bordering the White Rock Lake, and quickly found a blockade formed by several Dallas Police Department patrol cars. She was glancing around, looking for a way in, when a sharp rap on her car window brought her face-to-face with a striking uniformed blonde sporting reflective sunglasses, looking crisp and cool despite the fact it was already almost ninety degrees outside.

She wasn't sure how long she'd been staring when the officer rolled her hand and pointed at the window. She lowered the glass and summoned her ability to speak. "Hello, Officer."

"You're going to need to turn around. This part of the park is closed right now."

"I know. I heard the chatter on the scanner." Macy reached into the console between the seats and pulled out her press pass. There was a time when she'd been such an ever-present fixture at crime scenes, she hadn't needed to show her credentials, but clearly, she'd been out of the mix for too long. She held it out to the officer. "Not here as a voyeur, I promise. Were you the first officer on scene?"

The woman didn't answer, and her body language was intensely still, conveying no helpful information. Macy scanned her chest for a name badge, but it was obscured by the neon vest she was wearing. It was likely someone assigned to such a junior role of directing traffic at the crime scene didn't know any pertinent details, but she'd be crazy not to try to dig deeper. "Can you at least tell me the gender of the victim? Approximate age?"

She didn't expect any particular answer, but years of experience told her there were two ways to get the information she needed to craft a front-page story. Ask so many questions that the subject gets overwhelmed and starts blurting out answers, or fill the space between questions with so much silence, the subject was compelled to bridge the gaps with more information than they'd intended to share. Judging by the look on this woman's face, the many questions approach wasn't going to work, but she suspected the silent game wouldn't work either. "Can you tell me anything?"

The woman's face remained impassive. "You can stay, but you have to move your car. Nothing in the First Amendment says you get to block emergency vehicles because you're a journalist."

Macy gripped the steering wheel. "Fine." She threw the car into reverse and drove backward about a hundred feet and parked it in the grass, figuring the cops were too immersed in the crime scene to write her a ticket. She stuffed her phone into her messenger bag, threw it over her shoulder, and climbed out of her car. She looked over at where she'd been greeted by the officer in the vest who was talking to what looked like her superior. Neither one seemed to notice her, so she decided this was the perfect opportunity to do some detecting of her own.

She ducked behind her car and scouted out the area, deciding on a hunch to head to the wooded area where one of the tributaries fed into the lake. The ground was slightly wet and mud caked on her shoes, but by taking the long way around, she avoided the cops until she was right up on the scene.

She'd seen dead bodies before—in both photos and real life—but this was different because the scene before her conjured a memory that had changed her life.

The woman was young, probably in her early twenties. Fit and lean—easy to discern by the fact she was naked. She was probably a runner, but her bulging eyes and the taut tan rope around her neck were sure signs she'd never run again. Or do anything else for that matter. The fact she was hogtied was overkill, but Macy recognized it right away as a signature, and she shuddered to find her suspicions were true.

"What are you doing here?"

She turned to see the hot officer with the vest and her cohort standing behind her, looking indignant, but she didn't miss a beat. "Macy Moran with the *Dallas Gazette*. I have a few questions."

The blonde opened her mouth like she was going to say something, but the guy next to her, whose name badge read Sgt. Templeton, shot her a piercing glare, and she apparently thought better of it.

"Get the hell away from here." Templeton pointed to the area behind them. "This is an active crime scene and we have no comment at this time."

She followed them as they led her away from the scene. "Fine, but can you at least tell me which detective is assigned to this case?" When they didn't answer, she huffed, disappointed to be headed away from the action. "Come on, it's not like I'm not going to see whoever it is show up when they get here. Unless they're already here and I'll see them when I leave."

Templeton pointed to a spot several feet away. "Stay there and don't move." He signaled to the other officer and they walked over to one of the patrol cars.

"Hey, Macy, what are you doing here?"

She turned to see Rob Sturgess, the reporter from her paper who covered this beat headed toward them. "Hey, Rob. You just show up?"

"Very funny. I just heard it on the scanner. I repeat, what are you doing here?"

"I have a scanner too, but I guess I drive a faster car."

He strode closer and whispered. "It's not cool for you to show up like this."

"When you start covering your beat the way you should, I'll leave you to it. You're welcome to stick around, but I'm working an angle and I'm not leaving until I get a statement. I'll be happy to share it with you."

Macy looked up to see Templeton had left and the blonde was staring at them. "Play nice," she said to Rob in a low voice. "We're being watched."

"Don't tell me what to do. I've got this." He shot her a stinging look and strode over to Officer Blonde with his typical I'm so handsome I can get women to do whatever I want swagger.

She watched as he tried to make his play, but before he could get more than a few words out, he was interrupted by a shout from Templeton who was standing about twenty feet away.

"Ramsey. Over here."

All three of them looked over to the right where Templeton stood with a snarl on his face. He jabbed his finger at Rob. "No comment means no comment," he said. "Stay back and stay out of the way."

Rob ignored his command and walked over to him, but Macy backed away, years of experience telling her it was better not to push at this point. If she stuck around long enough, someone would be willing to talk, but it wasn't going to be this guy. A second later, she heard a voice over her shoulder, low and quiet. "It's too soon to know much, but it's definitively a homicide. You didn't hear it from me."

She suppressed her instinct to turn and look, but she knew it was the blond officer who'd spoken. What had Templeton called her? Ramsey. The name sounded familiar, and she checked her memory for a clue. It hit her in seconds. Officer Beck Ramsey. She'd been in the news lately for her role in an officer-involved shooting, but Macy had been so involved in the feature story that had been consuming her attention it took her a moment to conjure up the details. Her partner had done the shooting, but Beck had turned him in or something like that.

What was she doing working a murder scene if she was in the middle of an active investigation? She turned to ask exactly that, but the woman had walked away and all she saw was her back. While she was contemplating her next move, her phone buzzed again, repeatedly. A quick glance at the screen told her Jerry was growing increasingly impatient. She weighed her options. Instinct told her to blow him off, but practicality won out. If she didn't find a way to placate him, he could kill her feature story, and since that was pretty much all she cared about right now, the decision was made. She stared at Beck Ramsey's back as she receded into the distance. There was a story there, but it wasn't the one she wanted. Time to move on.

She waited until she pulled into the lot of the Starbucks at Casa Linda before she texted a reply to Jerry. *Sorry. Stopped to get coffee and ran into traffic. Be there soon.* Satisfied she'd put him off for a bit, she walked into the coffee shop to get evidence to support her little white lie. Ignoring the barista's recommendation of a drink with way too many descriptive phrases, she purchased two medium black coffees and stepped to the side. While she waited for her order, she did a visual sweep of the place, her ears tuning in to the random bits of conversation happening all around her. A couple in the corner was reviewing a real estate contract with a very young, but very well-dressed agent; a woman was applying an entire face of makeup using the tiniest mirror Macy had ever seen to guide her; and a twenty-something guy had brought his twenty-seven-inch iMac into the store and appeared to be setting up for the workday. She was shaking her head at the crazy level of randomness when something even more random happened.

She stared for a moment, unsure if her eyes were deceiving her. Convinced they weren't, she took a step toward the man who'd just placed his order and stepped over to wait near him. His hair was thinner and grayer than she remembered, and his posture was bent making him appear to be not as tall, but she was almost certain her mind wasn't playing tricks on her. "Wayne?"

He turned slowly toward her, his eyes scrunched in apparent confusion, but then his lips slid into a slow smile. "Macy? Wow. I can't believe it's you."

He opened his arms and Macy stepped into his embrace. Wayne Paxton had been her mentor when she'd started out at the paper as an intern, and she hadn't seen him since he'd moved back East years ago. "It's great to see you. Are you back for good or just visiting? How's Cathy? Is she with you?"

The smile remained, but his eyes darkened at the mention of his wife. "I'm back for good." His voice choked on the next words. "Cathy died a few months ago."

"Oh no, I'm so sorry to hear that." Macy had met Wayne's wife only once when she accompanied him to a Christmas party.

Cathy had barely said two words the entire evening, but based on the way Wayne doted on her, Macy knew her death had been a big blow. Her phone buzzed and she glanced at it out of habit. "Sorry, I'm running late, and Jerry is all over me about it."

"Silva's still there?"

"He is. Working us all to death." A thought struck her. "Hey, are you coming back to the paper?" The prospect of having his veteran expertise back in the newsroom gave her hope that maybe things at the office might shift back to the way they'd been before the Baxter Group had started eyeing the paper for purchase. Her mind started whirring with ways to convince Jerry they needed to hire Wayne back.

He shook his head. "I don't think so. I haven't been in the business for a while now. Too much has changed. I've got money saved up. I'll settle in and figure out my next move."

She wanted to stay. To catch up with him and hear what he'd been doing since he'd left Dallas and let him debrief about his grief, but if she didn't get to the office soon, no telling what dumb assignment Jerry would give her as punishment. "We should get together soon. I live about a mile from here and Louie's is still here," she said, referring to the dive pizza bar they used to frequent.

"Sure. That would be great. I'm living up in Plano though. Just in the old neighborhood seeing a friend." He raised his cup. "Cheers to a bonus friend sighting in the process."

A minute later, with his phone number typed into her phone, she left the Starbucks thinking she'd had a full day no matter what else happened. When she drove back by the lake, she wondered if Beck Ramsey was still there working the case, but she knew her musings were more about how good Ramsey looked in her uniform versus anything crime related. Focus, Moran, focus.

Chapter Two

Beck heard footsteps coming up quickly behind her, but she kept walking, certain the reporter was going to push her for more info. She'd already said more than she should, and she needed to bug out soon if she was going to make her hearing.

"Ramsey, hold up."

She reluctantly stopped at the sound of the familiar voice, and turned to face the commanding officer on scene, Sergeant Templeton. "Sir?"

He bent over at the waist, hands on his knees, and huffed from exertion. "Are you deaf? I've been yelling for you."

"Sorry, sir. I told Lansing I needed to go. Hearing's this afternoon."

His face twisted into a sour frown. She didn't need to tell him which hearing. Everyone knew her former partner Jack Staples's probable cause hearing was today, and she was the star witness. "Maybe you could do everyone a favor and sit it out."

As if. She didn't bother gracing his suggestion with a response, instead pointing at her phone. "Dispatch is sending out another patrol car to help cover. Gotta go."

She could hear him grunting an expletive as she walked away. She'd much rather stay here and blow off the hearing, but she didn't need to give the department another reason to eye her with suspicion. She couldn't unsee what Jack had done, and now that everyone knew about it, she had to go all in, or her fate would be even worse.

It took forever to get to her car, mostly because she had to walk past several other officers who demonstrated their distaste for her with disapproving stares. One of them—she didn't know his name—coughed "bitch" into his hand as she walked by, and it took every ounce of resistance she had not to fire off a retort, but it wouldn't change anything, and right now she wasn't interested in wasting the energy.

She was in her car and headed out of the park when her cell phone rang. "Ramsey here."

"Officer Ramsey, it's Lance Neely. Just checking in about the hearing this afternoon."

She rolled her eyes at the prosecutor's eagerness. Ready was a relative concept. "I'm good. Just headed to change and I'll be there."

"Judge Hernandez is pretty no-nonsense, so he's not going to let Staples's attorney beat up on you, and I'll be there to make sure things don't get out of hand."

"I know Hernandez," she said, unable to resist adding, "this isn't my first time appearing in court."

He laughed. "Sure, yeah, I know, but I'm guessing it's your first time testifying against a fellow officer. Am I right?"

"Correct." She hoped her clipped tone would curtail this conversation.

"I expect there will be plenty of spectators, which is not the norm for this kind of pro forma hearing, but I've read up on you and I think you'll be able to keep your cool."

"Thanks for the vote of confidence." She didn't bother hiding her sarcasm.

"Okay, then. I'll let you go."

She hung up without saying good-bye. She wasn't normally a rude person, but the events of the past month had edged out her ability to be civil under most circumstances. She drove around the lake and exited on Buckner Road, but instead of taking the turn toward the White Rock substation, she turned in the opposite direction and drove to her apartment in the Village. Normally, she'd change in a locker room at the station, but she didn't want to spend an extra minute in the company of colleagues who'd turned from friends to foes.

The Village was a sprawling set of apartment buildings, popular with college students and young Dallas singles. When she'd first moved in, she'd hated the place and vowed to move as soon as she found a complex with a less bustling atmosphere, but she'd come to enjoy the anonymity of living in such a large community. She was young enough to fit in but came and went with enough purpose not to call attention, even in uniform. The complex was known for hosting community events, and she'd avoided all of them. Other than the gay guys next door who tried to entice her with their weekly Wine Wednesdays, she didn't know a soul in the entire place.

Once inside, she shed her sweaty uniform and stood in the middle of her bedroom, under the ceiling fan, in her underwear. She closed her eyes and reveled in the cool breeze from the fan, dreading the idea of putting on another set of clothes in this heat. The last thing she wanted to do was show up in court and testify about anything, especially against her former partner, but she didn't have a choice.

She shed the rest of her clothes and took a quick shower. After she toweled off, she pulled a fresh uniform from the closet. She took her time getting dressed, making sure every button was polished and there wasn't a wrinkle in sight. She finished by tying her hair back into a tight French braid. She needed all the armor she could get today.

She was on her way to the courthouse when her phone dinged with an incoming text. Her brother, Liam. *Good luck today. Thinking about you.* She texted him back a thumbs up. At least she had one person in her corner.

When she parked in the lot next to the courthouse, she took a moment to center herself before going inside. She thought about the young woman they'd pulled off the trail by the lake that morning and she thought about Ben Aldridge, dying at her feet, less than two months ago. Unlike either one of them, she was alive and had a future ahead of her, no matter how uncertain.

She could do this. She had to do this, because if she couldn't, she would never be able to live with herself and she'd never be able to get past it. She adjusted her collar, got out of the car, and started the long walk to the courthouse entrance, praying she wouldn't run into any of her fellow officers along the way.

CHAPTER THREE

M acy was trading stares at her computer screen and the files on her desk when she heard a loud knock on her office door. She shoved her research into her desk drawer and yelled, "Come in." She needn't have bothered because her boss, Jerry Silva, already had the door open. "You have to stop doing that. What if I wasn't dressed?"

"Then you'd be having a helluva lot more fun than me." He tossed a file onto her desk.

"What's that?" she asked, pointing a finger like it was an insect.

"I need you to cover a hearing this afternoon. That DPD officer Beck Ramsey, who ratted out her partner, is testifying at a hearing in Hernandez's court. Jeff was covering it, but his kid's sick and he has to go pick him up at school."

Macy perked up at the mention of Beck's name, but even the prospect of more eye candy wasn't enough to entice her away from her current project. "Yawn. It's a hearing. Can't you send one of the other kids to cover?" she asked, referring to the junior reporters who would jump at the chance to get words in print. She vaguely remembered what that kind of enthusiasm was like. "I'm deep into research on the anniversary piece."

"You've been doing 'research,'" he used actual air quotes, "for weeks. I can't sell research to the board as a reason to keep you around. You know how much pressure we're under to show a profit if we want to keep from getting bought out and sold for parts. You need actual words formed into a compelling story for me if you want to keep your job. And I'd like to keep you around," he added, kind of softening the blow. "Besides, Rob tells me you showed up on a dead body call out at White Rock this morning. He was pretty pissed, thinking I'd sent you to scoop him."

She shrugged. "I was right there when the call came over the scanner. Beat Rob there, by the way. I figured you'd appreciate my initiative. Besides, he'd have to actually do some real reporting for me to be able to scoop him."

"Let's just say I'm a little suspicious of your so-called initiative. Is this more of your 'research'?"

"Don't use air quotes on me. I'm always looking for an angle. The call was about a body at White Rock Lake, so of course I'm going to check it out. Something wrong with that?"

"Not by me." He shoved the folder at her again. "But today I need you to look for angles somewhere else. Sure, it's just a hearing, but if you work it right, it's a wedge into a bigger story about what makes a cop turn on one of their own."

"Easy answer—it was the right thing to do. Didn't her partner shoot an innocent guy?"

"Sure, but it happens all the time. Not everyone speaks up. Besides, have you seen her?"

Macy reached across the desk and opened the file. The picture inside was nothing more than a still of Beck in uniform, and she resisted the urge to comment she looked even better in person. "You think I'm going to fall for your attempt to lure me away from what I'm doing to go see Officer Model here testify? And quit objectifying women or I'll tell your wife."

"Like she'd care." He pointed at the file. "She's news and it's your job to cover the news." His voice took on a pleading tone. "Seriously, Mace. I need you to do this. We're short-staffed this week, and I rarely ever insist."

It was true, he didn't. Mostly because he knew it was futile. Award-winning reporters like her could find other work, even go out on their own in the current market where everyone with a smartphone could host their own blog, and while the board might not want to spend the money it took to fund the really big stories, they loved the accolades when those stories won awards. She pulled the file closer and set aside the picture of Beck Ramsey. Ramsey had turned in her partner, Jack Staples, after a fatal shooting of a twenty-year-old young man they'd pulled over for allegedly driving erratically. Staples had insisted the kid had resisted arrest, but Ramsey refuted his story. Staples had failed to turn on his body cam, and the view from Ramsey's wasn't definitive, making her the key witness. Yes, what she'd done was the right thing to do, but it was rare to see a veteran cop turn on one of their own, no matter what the offense. Macy couldn't help but be intrigued.

"Okay," she said. "I'll do it." She reached for the file. "You know you're the last person in the newsroom to keep using paper files?"

"I'll stop when you punks stop crashing the network with your Tik Toks and Facetimes."

Macy groaned. "Let's grab lunch soon and I'll teach you how not to talk like someone's great-granddad." She shooed him away. "Now go so I can read the file."

He started toward the door, yelling over his shoulder. "You mean the paper file?"

He'd barely cleared the door and she was engrossed in the material. Beck Ramsey had started her career with the Austin Police Department after obtaining a degree in criminal justice from UT and had transferred to Dallas a few years ago. She'd been decorated several times and had recently taken the detective's exam. If nothing else, her testimony should be interesting.

She reached for her messenger bag and took a moment to appreciate the rich leather that had developed a lush patina with age. Wayne had gifted her the bag when she'd graduated from Richards University, and she carried it with her on every reporting gig like a lucky talisman. She made a mental note to give him a call, and then loaded her phone and Beck's file—apparently, they were on a first-name basis now—into the bag and left the office.

The courthouse was just on the other side of downtown, but the trip could take five minutes or thirty, depending on traffic. She made it in fifteen and pulled into the parking garage next to the building, praying the usually full garage would have an open spot considering afternoon hearings were rare. On the second swing through the floors, she managed to tuck her Mini Cooper between two giant SUVs. She took the stairs down to the side entrance for the courthouse and rushed her way to the security line, thankful to find it almost empty. Despite the lack of a line, the guards were still painfully slow, and she barely held back the urge to yell at them to hurry. Finally free, she raced to the courtroom, but a quick glance at the camera crew filming just outside told her the hearing was already in progress.

"Hey, Macy, you lost?"

She rolled her eyes at Joan Brown, the courthouse correspondent for one of the local news outlets and a former flame. "Thought I'd show up and see what's shakin'."

"Tired of missing out on the fun stuff?"

Macy shrugged, refusing to be goaded about the fact she wasn't in the thick of courthouse reporting anymore. "All a matter of perspective."

"Seriously, where's Jeff?"

"Kid trouble. Besides, this used to be my beat." She pointed at the small windows on the courtroom door. "Anything happening yet?"

"Judge just took the bench. You better get a seat if you want to hear the bombshells."

"You think there's going to be some?"

"How often do you see one of their own crossing the line?" Joan leaned close. "Besides, she's super-hot. Count yourself lucky for drawing this assignment. There are worse ways to spend the afternoon than sitting around staring at a hot cop."

Was she the only one who was interested in an actual story more than the opportunity to leer at Beck Ramsey? "Yeah, okay." She waved at Joan and pushed through the doors. The courtroom was packed—unusual for an afternoon any day of the week, but especially a Friday when juries wrapped up and judges and prosecutors ditched early to head to happy hour. The first thing Macy noticed was the composition of the audience. Cops in uniform were packed into one side, behind defense counsel table, and the rows behind the prosecutor were full of what appeared to be subdued, for now, protestors, judging by the many T-shirts with slogans like Black Lives Matter and Defund the Police. Hernandez, a Democrat, was way more lenient about political fashion statements than most judges, but she was surprised he was allowing such a display for what was sure to be a contentious hearing.

She slid into a tight spot in the back row and pulled out a pencil and notebook, eschewing the notes app on her phone for analog since the presence of phones made bailiffs edgy. She scribbled a few first impressions. *Cops and protestors seated on either side of the aisle like a wedding party, except at the end of the day no one would be getting married. In fact, instead of bringing these two sides together, whatever happened here today was likely to widen the divide between them.*

She wrote a few more paragraphs, and then tapped her pencil on the notebook while she envisioned Jerry cutting her flowery notes to a fraction of their length and reminded herself she was here to report on a simple story. Just the facts. She'd been writing features for so long, it was hard to remember to pare her account down to fit a simple metro piece, but it was a good exercise for keeping her writing tight and brief. She jotted down a few words to capture the feeling in the room—tense, taut, anxious—and then stared at the bench with the rest of the crowd, captured by the growing fever pitch.

"Call your first witness," Judge Hernandez said, staring fiercely at the gallery as if daring anyone to make a sound. He needn't have worried. The air in the room was sucked away when ADA Neely rose from his chair. "The state calls Detective Rebecca Ramsey."

Beck Ramsey, the only person seated in the front row behind the prosecutor, stood and started walking to the witness stand to the right of the judge. She settled into the seat confidently, like she'd occupied it dozens of times, which she probably had. Nothing remarkable here, but when she looked up and faced the packed room, Macy sucked in a breath at the sight of her eyes, no longer hidden behind reflective lenses. Wow. Deep, dark brown and decidedly fierce. Even from the back of the room, she could feel the force of the unwavering gaze, and when Beck Ramsey scanned the room, she sent up a mental wave: look at me, look at me.

And Beck did. A long, hard stare that shook her to her core.

CHAPTER FOUR

B eck tore her gaze from the soulful eyes of the reporter in the back row, telling herself it was a coincidence she'd seen her twice in one day. She faced the crowded room and tried to drown out the voices in her head telling her she should run. She'd spent the past month living as a pariah among her brothers and sisters on the force, but she wasn't ready to embrace the hero worship of the protestors who'd filled the rows in the gallery to get a glimpse at their new poster girl. Ultimately, none of it really mattered. This wasn't her first time testifying in court, but she suspected it would be one of her last.

She'd done her job. It was that simple and that complex, but the consequences were life-altering. Her former partner, Jack Staples, a man she'd shared meals and conversation with, a man she'd trusted to have her back and with whom she'd trusted her life on numerous occasions, was sitting next to his lawyer a few feet away, staring her down with a flank of fellow officers in the rows behind him, all clearly signaling who they thought was on the right side of the law. She hadn't spoken directly to Jack since a few days after the shooting, and it had long since become too late to bridge the gap between them. The difference between friendship and fatality had become clear in less than ten seconds, but the effects would linger for the rest of her life.

"Do you swear to tell the truth, so help you God?"

She took a moment to return Jack's stare before she turned to the judge and injected her voice with an extra boost of confidence. "Yes. I do."

The prosecutor, Lance Neely, remained seated while he took her through the preliminary round of questions. This was a hearing, not a trial, and there was no jury to impress, but beyond that there was nothing casual about this proceeding, and she remained tense even on the light background stuff.

"What was the exact message from the 911 dispatcher?"

"Another motorist had seen a car matching Mr. Aldridge's vehicle, driving westbound on Highway 635 between Central Expressway and Preston Road. The dispatcher told us the car was swerving between lanes. We'd just finished our meal break at Central and Coit, so we took the call."

"And what did you do next?"

She took him through their drive, switching lanes across Interstate 635 in an attempt to locate the reported erratic driver. "After about ten minutes, we pulled in behind a vehicle matching the description given by the 911 caller."

"Did you immediately pull the vehicle over?"

Here we go. She took a deep breath. "We did not. We stayed back a couple of car lengths and followed the vehicle, observing its driving patterns."

"And was the in-car camera operational at this time?"

She shifted in her seat. "I don't know."

"Why is that, Officer Ramsey?"

This would be the first cut. Would it hurt her more than him or the other way around? "I asked Officer Staples to turn on the camera when we first observed the vehicle."

"Did you see him turn it on?"

"No. Later…after…it was determined that nothing was recorded either while we were on the road or at the scene." She held up her hands. "If he turned it on, it wasn't working. I didn't know that at the time." There. She'd given up the best bit of reasonable doubt she could. About the stop anyway, but the rest…

"Who made the decision to initiate lights and sirens and pull Mr. Aldridge over?"

That was easy. "Officer Staples did."

"Did you disagree with his assessment?"

She started to parse the question. She hadn't agreed. They'd observed nothing other than a car driving down the highway. No taillights out, no speeding, no signs of erratic driving. Other than the call to 911, they had nothing in the way of reasonable suspicion to pull him over and she'd said so to Jack at the time. "We discussed it, but Jack...Officer Staples made the decision to initiate the stop citing safety for the driver of the car."

"You mean, Mr. Aldridge?"

She got the irony. She really did. Mr. Aldridge was dead and buried in the big cemetery off Forest Lane with no one left to tell his story. He should've at least gotten his day in court, but no—the guy who gunned him down was the only one getting access to justice. "Yes, Mr. Aldridge. Officer Staples specifically mentioned the community care-taking provision."

"Tell the court what you mean by that."

She hated this part. The judge knew the law and the prosecutor asking her to repeat it was for show. "An officer as part of their duty to 'serve and protect' may stop and assist an individual whom they believe is in need of help."

"And you disagreed that this provision in the law supported the reason for the stop?"

She glanced at the judge, wishing he would do something to stop the repetition, but he seemed as riveted with anticipation as everyone else in the room. "I didn't personally observe any circumstances that led me to believe it was necessary."

"Thank you. Now—"

She couldn't resist adding. "But I also didn't believe it would be harmful."

Neely glared at her for a moment before he caught the judge looking at him and then his expression morphed into an indulgent smile. "You didn't believe it would be harmful to make the stop at the time, right? When you were still driving behind Mr. Aldridge's car? But you eventually changed your opinion on that point, correct?"

She could hear the gotcha in his voice, underscoring what she'd known all along—she had no friends on either side. The only thing she could do now was answer as honestly and completely as possible and hope it was over soon. "Correct."

His next few questions took her through what happened after the stop. Both she and Jack had gotten out of the car. She'd walked around to the passenger side and shone a flashlight inside while Jack had approached the driver's window. She heard most of the conversation that had gone down, but nothing that supported Jack's decision to demand that Aldridge exit his vehicle.

"Did he exit the car when ordered to do so?"

"He opened the door and started to get out."

"What happened then?"

She'd replayed the event a thousand times. The first few times had been a tangled mess of movements and shouting and confusion, but over time the threads had started to unravel and now she could see the Technicolor short film play out in her head and she'd memorized every moment. "He had one leg out of the car and was starting to stand up. His right hand swung slowly toward Jack, like this." She raised her hand from her lap and mimicked the motion she'd seen. "Officer Staples yelled for him to place his hands in the air."

"Did Mr. Aldridge comply?"

He hadn't. Not immediately, but it was kind of hard to place your hands in the air when you were using them to push your way out of the car. The conflicting demands might have been the cause for confusion, if confusion was what it really was. "He didn't at first."

"How did Officer Staples respond?"

"He drew his weapon and again shouted for Mr. Aldridge to show his hands." She paused, replaying the details in her head. He'd whipped his head around, clearly afraid and unsure how to deal with the conflicting demands. "He lifted his left arm and he extended his right hand toward Officer Staples."

"Was there anything in his hand that you could see at the time?"

"Yes."

"Could you make out what it was?"

It was hard to separate what she knew now from what she knew then, no matter how hard she'd worked to draw a line between the two, but she was convinced her memory was accurate. "Yes, it was a phone."

"Why do you think that was the case?"

"I could see the screen light up when he lifted it from the seat." She'd never forget the image on the screen—a small child, with a big smile, playing on a jungle gym. Such specific detail for the few seconds of time she'd had to see it, but the picture was burned in her memory as a symbol of the loss caused on that fateful night.

"What happened next?"

His job was so easy. All he had to do was prompt her, question and answer, to end her career and everything that defined her. "Officer Staples shouted 'gun' and he fired his weapon."

"Do you know how many times he fired?"

In the chaos of the moment, it could have been once or fifty. But she'd read the report since then and now knew it had been five. Five loud, quick shots fired directly into the center of Mr. Aldridge's chest. Five shots that ensured he'd never be pulled over or harassed by the police again. Five shots that robbed the little boy in the picture of a father. Robbed his wife of a husband. His parents of a son.

"Five. He fired five times."

A hush fell over the courtroom. She wasn't sure why since she hadn't said much of anything yet that hadn't already been reported in the news. She surveyed the crowd of cops, daring all of them to meet her eyes. Few did and probably because they knew what was coming next.

"At any time from the moment you and Officer Staples made the stop to the moment Officer Staples fired his weapon, did you see Mr. Aldridge in possession of a gun?"

Neely injected a ton of portent in the question, leaning forward, staring into her eyes, his voice deeper than it had been moments ago. But she wasn't buying into the drama. She turned in her seat and delivered her answer directly to the judge. "No, I did not."

When he finally passed her as a witness, Jack's attorney sprang out of his seat and waved his hand in the air for emphasis. "Is it your contention that just because you didn't see a gun, it wasn't there at all?"

"No."

"Well, I'm certain that's what Mr. Neely wants this judge and potentially a jury to infer."

Jack shouldn't have hired such a jackass to represent him. "I have no idea what Mr. Neely wants, but if the judge or anyone else wants to know the truth about this case, here it is. We shouldn't have made the stop, we didn't need to ask Mr. Aldridge to get out of his car, and I think we can infer from the fact that no gun or any other weapon was found at the scene that my recollection is correct. Mr. Aldridge never had a gun."

She leaned back as much as the stiff chair would allow and crossed her arms. She didn't care if the press depicted her as pissed off. She *was* pissed off and she knew she had to stop caring so much about what other people thought about her if she was ever going to recover from this ordeal.

The rest of the questions were a blur, all designed to lay a foundation for either side at trial. She responded honestly, but kept her answers tight and lean, her only goal to get this over with as soon as possible. When the hearing was over, the judge continued Jack on his current bond, and the minute he gaveled the session closed, she started to bolt from her seat, but Neely motioned for her to stay as he walked toward her.

"Let the bailiff clear the room and then he'll show you out the back. You don't want to wind up in the middle of this mess."

She watched the protestors pushing toward the cops as they funneled out of the room. He was right, but his admonition was one more unpleasant reminder of how much her life had changed in the last month and how much more it was likely to change as things went on. "What's next after this?"

"We'll have a few court sittings to try to work something out, and if we can't, we'll set a trial date."

"He's not going to take a plea."

"He might."

"I'm telling you he won't. Jack doesn't back down. He may know in his heart of hearts that he was wrong, but he's not the kind of guy who likes to admit it. And I'm assuming you'd make giving up his TCLOSE certification as a condition of any deal, right?"

"Probably."

He didn't make eye contact and she knew he was hedging. "No cop is going to voluntarily give up their entire career. He's ten years in."

"He could be looking at life if he gets a guilty verdict."

"You and I both know juries don't give cops the max if they convict at all. He's going to know it too and he's going to take his chances at trial."

Neely clasped her on the shoulder. "Then I guess it's a good thing I have a really good eyewitness."

She shrugged out of his grasp and stepped away as the bailiff approached. "Yeah, whatever." Without waiting for a response, she followed the bailiff out the back door of the courtroom and down a hall past the judge's chambers to an exit about twenty yards from where the rest of the courtroom crowd had dumped out. She wished she'd thought to bring street clothes to change into to make it more likely she would blend into the crowd, but she had a meeting with her lieutenant in an hour and the best thing she could do right now was to get out of here as quickly as possible.

She'd turned the corner, toward the hallway when she heard a voice call out to her.

"Officer Ramsey?"

Instinctively, she turned toward the sound, but she didn't answer. She recognized the woman as the one from the lake this morning, the one who'd been seated in the back row of the courtroom. The one who'd caught her eye and, she hated to admit, piqued her interest, despite her profession. And that was the only reason she slowed her pace. She glanced around, but they were alone.

The woman stuck out her hand. "I'm Macy Moran with the *Dallas Gazette*. We met this morning. May I walk with you?"

"Free country." Beck paused for a moment. A pretty reporter was still a reporter. Ultimately, she decided to ignore Macy's outstretched hand and kept walking, picking up the pace and hoping she could outdistance the shorter woman.

Macy didn't seem deterred by her fast pace. "I was hoping I could get a statement from you."

"You were in court. I'm sure you got plenty of fodder to use in there."

"You were partners with Jack Staples for years. Were you friends too?"

Beck lost her gait at the unexpected question. Plenty of reporters had shouted questions at her since the shooting, but they all asked the usual stuff, mostly wanting a minute breakdown of every aspect of the traffic stop and everything that followed. Their persistence had made her persona non grata at her apartment complex, and whenever things with the case ramped up, she'd resorted to bunking in at her brother's place to duck the throngs of journalists who would not let the story die. Yet not a one of them had thought to ask her if she and Jack had been friends, and Macy's question stabbed her to the core. She'd always considered Jack a friend, but the public shunning she'd received from him and the rest of the force signaled she'd been dead wrong, which led her to question what else she'd been wrong about over the course of her career.

But she wasn't going to discuss her life, her feelings, with a stranger, especially not one who was likely to print the personal details of her life in the pages of her paper. She answered with the words her union rep had made her practice over and over again. "No comment."

Undeterred, Macy followed her out of the building, into the garage, and to her car. The walk was strange since neither one of them said another word the whole way. When they reached her Jeep, Beck reached into her pocket, fished out her keys, and pressed the button to unlock the door. She turned to face Macy. "Are you going to follow me home? Because I have a couple of stops along the way and I wouldn't want you to get lost, although I'm sure you know where I live along with everything else about me."

Macy jammed her notebook into her bag and cocked her head. "I doubt that. I'm thinking whatever spurred you to speak up about your partner of many years is a well that runs deep, and even Jack Staples, the man who rode alongside you all that time, never saw it coming. I can figure out the rest, but the thing I really want to know is, was this the first time you witnessed something like this from him, or was it just the straw that broke the camel's back?"

Whoa. She hadn't seen that coming. Chalk it up to one more instance of her instincts failing her. She shook her head and got in the car, gripping the steering wheel tightly to ground herself. To everyone else she'd either been the traitor or the hero, but to Macy Moran, she was apparently nothing more than a coward who'd finally had enough. Maybe that was true. She wasn't sure, but did know this: Macy Moran was trouble and she was going to steer clear.

Chapter Five

*G*reat angle. I knew you were the right one for this story.
Macy deleted Jerry's email as fast as she'd read it. The story she'd written about Beck Ramsey was a distraction. Ramsey was a cop with cop instincts and cop tendencies and there was nothing newsworthy about that. She'd probably protected Jack Staples's homicidal tendencies until it became unbearable for her, but a life might have been saved if she'd spoken up sooner. Every other paper in town was casting Ramsey as either a hero or pariah, but rarely was the truth that simple. Which brought her back to the feature piece she'd been working on for the past six months, the one Jerry was convinced she should abandon but knew that if he ordered her off it, she'd walk out.

Ten years ago, a ruthless killer had started a violent spree, claiming five victims from various walking/biking trails in the Dallas city limits. The victims were all female and in their early twenties and their deaths had taken place over the course of a year. The times of the deaths had varied—three in the pre-sunrise dark and two just after dusk. Their bodies had been found in various stages of decomposition, from one day to a week, by a variety of different people: a hiker chasing her dog who'd slipped his leash, a fisherman looking for the perfect cove to cast his line, a kayaker cutting through the brush to put in on a portion of the lake not as crowded as the rest. Each victim had been bounded, gagged, and strangled with a piece of plain hemp rope. And the fifth victim had been her best friend, Lauren Webb.

The press at the time had dubbed the perpetrator the Parks and Rec Killer. The moniker had stuck, but there had never been a face to put to the name. Somehow, he'd managed to lure his victims off one of the many walking/biking trails around the area, kill them, and leave them for dead in the ditches and byways mere yards from public view without being detected. The police had assumed the women went with him willingly, à la Ted Bundy, which was how he avoided detection in the initial capture, but how had he committed such violent crimes without anyone suspecting what was going on?

A source at the police department had told her the police had initially questioned a suspect, but it didn't go anywhere. With no eyewitnesses, no leads from the simple, generic tools of the murder, and only trace amounts of DNA that had never been matched to anyone in the system, the investigation had seemed futile, and within a few months after Lauren's death, the police had moved on, relegating the dormant Parks and Rec Killer files to the other unsolved cases that didn't merit more resources since the danger had disappeared. If he wasn't still killing, their efforts could be put to better use stopping active criminals from their evil pursuits.

But dormant didn't mean dead, and Macy had always suspected the killer was lying in wait for the perfect opportunity to resume his spree. Or maybe he had already. Over the course of the past ten years, she'd spent her free time chatting in social media groups, searching online law enforcement databases, and scouring media outlets for any clues the Parks and Rec Killer had resumed his activities elsewhere. Lead after lead had gone nowhere, but last week when she'd heard the call over the radio about the dead body at White Rock Lake she'd gone on high alert, because the canon of serial killer knowledge was clear—bloodlust didn't merely disappear. That, coupled with the memory of her own, very personal loss, drove her to keep the story alive and now, on the eve of the anniversary of what appeared to be the killer's last murderous act, she was determined to publish a feature-length piece designed to bring the story back into the spotlight. Gruesome as the thought might be, if the killer was back at it, the likelihood of publication was even higher.

She picked up her phone to set a reminder to contact Claire Hanlon, the detective who'd been assigned to the White Rock case, for an update, but before she could type the note, her phone buzzed with an incoming text.

Quit being radio silent. We need to plan for Sunday.

It was Harrison, one of her best friends, and he was referring to Pride.

I may have to work.

Nope. Not how this goes. Pick you up at eleven. Donna will save our spot.

She hovered over the keys, crafting a half dozen different replies that all ended with *I can't make it*, but she knew skipping out wasn't an option and ultimately decided to give in. *Fine.*

The reminder of the past made her feel claustrophobic. She carried her phone with her and walked through the newsroom, passing by the desks of young reporters working on getting their stories in under deadline. There weren't many. The board had instructed management to slim down staff to buffer the bottom line and make the paper more palatable for potential purchasers, and many had been sent off to work from home so they could lease out half the space. She got it. The economics of news didn't work in a world where there was so much online content for free, even if more than half of it was unvetted dog shit. She'd managed to hang on to her salary and her tiny little office in the building, but with every passing day came the possibility she'd have to compromise and start composing unvetted clickbait. She wasn't going to do it. Not ever. The very idea caused her throat to close and her skin to burn, which, in turn, made her want to run. She gave in to the urge and walked briskly out of the building, gasping when she reached the outside air.

Downtown Dallas during the day was a bustling place, even with the early onset of high temperatures. The paper was only a block from Klyde Warren Park, and Macy slowed her walk to take in the ambiance of a city putting on a good face to hide its darker bits. Today was one of the better showings. A quartet from the arts magnet high school was playing at one end of the park and a group was taking a yoga class at the other end. In between, a dozen food trucks lined the edge, offering up an amazing array of choices. She often strolled the park at lunch, but she normally brought her own packed lunch. Today she was unencumbered by her usual turkey sandwich and free to feed her cravings. She watched the trucks to see which one had the biggest line, and she queued up behind the crowd at Easy Slider.

She carried her paper plate crowded with two small but well-stuffed burgers to a nearby bench and dove in, deliberating leaving her phone in her pocket so she could eat and people watch in peace. As if on cue, a group of businessmen walked in front of her holding tacos in their outstretched hands to avoid dribbling salsa onto their fussy suits. They'd be better off in one of the many steakhouses, dining on white tablecloths with fancy waiters, but she wasn't here to judge, only to observe.

A few minutes later, she spotted a cop standing a few feet away, turned in the other direction. She was tall and wore her blond hair in a braid. Could it possibly be? She willed the woman to turn around, and seconds later she did, but Macy was instantly disappointed at the unfamiliar face. She wasn't sure why she was surprised. Beck Ramsey wasn't going to be able to simply return to patrol. Not for a while anyway. Chances were good that after the damning testimony she'd given at the hearing, the department had her riding a desk, shuffling papers to stay busy, if not relevant.

Macy finished off her food and found a trash can to dispose of the plate. On her way back to the office, she spotted another female cop with her back turned. Another blonde, sans braid. The officer waved and smiled in her direction which told her right away it wasn't Beck. No, Beck hadn't been pleased with the press attention and she'd made it perfectly clear she'd prefer they all left her alone. Macy had no problem with that. The best stories came from witnesses who hadn't been coerced but were voluntarily helping out. Pressing Beck for a story again right now would likely drive her completely away. She wasn't sure why she cared about that, but she did, and it probably had something to do with those sad but beautiful brown eyes that had captivated her at the hearing last week. Stupid really since she didn't know Beck at all and people were rarely what they seemed to be.

Beck stared at the screen on her cell phone, unable to believe what she was reading. She'd had a two-second conversation with Macy Moran and not a bit of it was about the shooting, yet Moran had determined she was a codependent enabler of her psychopath ex-partner. Fucking reporters.

"Hey, Ramsey, Lieutenant Coy wants to see you in his office."

She tore her gaze away from the article to look at the guy riding the desk. "Yeah, okay. I'll be right there."

She jabbed at her phone to make Moran's story disappear, and then took a moment to clear her head. Her lieutenant didn't need to see her pissed off—it would be just one more thing to add to the list of reasons not to put her back out in the field. Like she needed any more. She took a few deep breaths, following the only decent advice she'd received from the department shrink, and then made her way to his office. She rapped on the doorframe.

"Come in and have a seat. And shut the door."

Great. This was going to be one of *those* conversations. She closed the door behind her and sat down on the edge of the seat in front of his desk, tense and ready.

He tossed aside the file in his hand and faced her. "Two things."

She waited, not interested in guessing her fate. He knew her well enough to nod and keep talking. "You passed your detective exam." He reached into his desk drawer and pulled out a box and slid it across the desk.

She hesitated before reaching for it. She'd imagined this moment many, many times, but in her head, it had carried much more momentum and celebration than the deadpan delivery of her lieutenant handing her a hunk of metal.

"It's yours, you may as well take it."

He didn't mean any harm with his words, but the casual delivery made it official. She'd been promoted and it meant nothing up against the position she was in for turning in Jack. Fine. But she'd earned the shield and she'd be damned if she was going to pass it up. She reached for the box but didn't open it, merely clenching it in her fist while she waited for whatever else he wanted to discuss. "You said there was something else."

"You've been assigned to the cold case squad. Take the rest of the day off and report to Sergeant Mendoza tomorrow morning."

Her head spun as his words slowly penetrated. It wasn't unusual to be transferred to a different division after making detective, but the cold case squad? What a joke. She was being promoted and shoved aside to examine files no one cared about anymore. What an appropriate end to her career. She pushed herself to her feet. "Fine. I'll clear out my locker and go."

She reached the door before he said another word.

"Ramsey?"

She glanced over her shoulder. "Sir?"

"For what it's worth, you did the right thing. No one here is going to say that where anyone else can hear, but you should hear it from me."

"You know what? I did do the right thing, but apparently, I'm going to pay for it because despite what I believed, that's not what we're about."

"That's not true."

"It is." She raised her hands in surrender. "I give up trying to understand it. The only thing I can do now is stick around and be a thorn in the side of everyone who thinks Jack Staples is a standup guy who did the right thing. You want to do me a solid? How about putting a word in to keep me from ending my career on the cold case squad?"

"I hate to say this, but it's probably the best place for you right now."

He was right and she knew it. With every other cop on the force gunning for her, she wouldn't be able to do her job knowing backup would be questionable at best, but it didn't make the conclusion sting any less. She left his office and packed her locker. It was noon on a Wednesday, and she had an entire afternoon to burn. She loaded her stuff in her Jeep and called her brother, Liam, as she pulled out of the parking lot at the station.

"Hey, sis. Everything okay?"

"Can I not call you just for the hell of it?"

"Under normal circumstances, yes. But lately…"

"Yeah, I know. Can I buy you lunch?"

"No, but I can buy you lunch. Name the place and I'll meet you there."

"If it's okay with you, can we meet at home, uh, your place." She'd been staying with him so much lately, her subconscious apparently assumed it was a permanent situation. "I'm about fifteen minutes away."

"Perfect. I'll order a pizza and it'll be ready by the time you get here."

They hung up and she turned east to head toward Deep Ellum. Liam owned a small ad agency in an old warehouse he'd converted into office space. He kept half of the ground floor and rented out the rest to a popular pizza joint and lived on the top floor in a swank industrial apartment.

She pulled into the open parking space in the back he reserved for personal guests and walked around to the front of the building. Liam's staff knew her well and she was on friendly terms with everyone, but she hadn't been to the office since before the shooting. Now, when they looked up as she entered, she couldn't help but wonder if she was imagining the knowing looks and shifting glances. She took a deep breath and pushed through.

"Thank God you're here. I'm starving." Liam burst into the room and wrapped her up in a bear hug, likely as much a display of genuine affection as a signal to the rest that she had his total support no matter what they might have read in the papers. "Say hi to the gang." He kept one arm around her as he spun her to see his tight-knit crew.

Wanda and Larry and Jill waved in her direction and called out hellos, and she waved back. "Hey, everybody. Whatcha working on?"

"Plant-based Spam," Wanda said, her face deadpan. "It's the new green meat. You like?"

"Spam or that pitch?"

"Either. They're both imaginary. Just trying to see how it flies."

Wendy was weird but she meant well, and according to Liam, she was amazing at coming up with creative campaigns. "Okay. Well, not a fan of Spam, but I like the plant-based angle."

"She's jacking with you, Beck. There's no Spam here, although I'm so hungry, I'd probably bust into a can right now." He grabbed her arm and pulled her toward the door. "Let's grab that pizza."

They strolled next door in companionable silence. Beck knew Liam wasn't going to force her to talk until she was ready, but the longer she went without sharing, the more likely it was she would stuff her feelings and keep her news to herself. They walked into the restaurant next door, and he pointed to the to-go counter. "You want to take it back to my apartment?"

She glanced around the room, The place was busy, but she didn't see any familiar faces. "We can eat here." She snagged a table while he grabbed their order. When he joined her with the food, she blurted out. "I got my detective shield today."

Liam's face lit up with a big smile. "Holy shit, Beck, that's great news."

"I guess so."

He cocked his head. "What aren't you telling me?"

"They assigned me to the cold case squad. I start there tomorrow."

"And that's a bad thing?"

"It's where detectives go to die, not where they start their careers. I finally get my shield and it's meaningless. I'll be counting the years to retirement surrounded by boxes of unsolvable cases that no one cares about anymore. What's the point?"

"That really sucks. Can you appeal?"

She laughed. "No such thing. Besides, the last thing I want to do right now is buck the system any further. Who knows where they'd reassign me next time?"

Liam nodded and pointed at the pizza box. "How about a slice to celebrate the promotion, even if it sucks?"

Beck's stomach rumbled as if on cue and they both laughed. They spent the next few minutes devouring their food, while Liam steered the conversation away from police work. "We're planning an open house at the office next month. Clients, neighbors, anyone who might need ad work. You in to help me plan?"

"Sure," she said, trying not to feel resentful about the muted celebration of her promotion, but considering the circumstances, there wasn't anything to celebrate. Throwing herself into someone else's party planning might be the perfect distraction. "I doubt I'll have long hours in the dead case files, so I should have plenty of free time to help out."

He reached across and stole a pepperoncini off of her plate. "You know, you might have the perfect opportunity to become a superstar with this promotion."

"Interesting theory. Based on what?"

"Come on, don't you ever watch *Dateline*, *20/20*? You could solve the unsolvable. Make the cold case heat up again. You might get a medal."

"Yeah no." She appreciated his enthusiasm, but it wasn't catching. "It doesn't work that way. Those shows feature cold cases that are one in a million. The truth is if the trail dried up, it's probably dead for good."

"Maybe. But you didn't become a cop because it was easy. You wanted to help people. Remember how you used to try on Mom's uniform and parade around the house?"

They both fell silent at the mention of their mother, and Beck cast about for a way to change the subject. "You're cute when you're being idealistic."

"You used to be."

He was right. Once upon a time, she'd been idealistic too. She'd wanted to be a cop since before she ever really understood exactly what it meant besides the cool uniform and badge. For years after she joined the force, she managed to retain the idealism of her youth, despite the blows life had dealt. But this incident and the subsequent abandonment of her brothers and sisters in blue had broken her, and she'd never recapture the hope and dreams of the work she'd once had.

"I don't think I can be anymore." The confession was hard coming, but the minute the words left her lips, she knew they were true. She'd try, but she didn't hold out hope. Her career was over, and a part of her died knowing that was true.

CHAPTER SIX

Macy pulled up to the house and took a moment to sketch the facade in her notebook. A quaint Craftsman, small but in this part of town with real estate prices on the rise it was probably worth close to half a mil. The porch was tiny but well-loved with lush green plants and a padded rocker. Wind chimes tinkled lightly, loud enough to be heard, but not in an annoying way. She added a few final details before shutting her notebook and carefully placing the pencil in the loop. She'd snap a photo too, but she preferred to draw things, even if her abilities were amateur, as that helped her solidify her ideas for the story.

She rang the bell and waited, enjoying the scent of fresh bread wafting through the air. When the door finally opened, she offered her most engaging smile to the man standing in front of her, hoping he wouldn't slam it shut when he found out who she was. "Mr. Silver?"

"I can't talk now. I'm baking," he said curtly.

"And it smells fantastic." The smile was starting to hurt, but she pressed on. "My name is Macy Moran. I was hoping I could talk to you about Janelle."

"Baking," he said, as if the single word explained all things.

He started to shut the door, but she called out, "Don't you want to find out who killed her?" Indelicate, she knew, but she'd been waiting years to get an opportunity to speak to him. "I can help," she added, hoping to soften the blow.

"You from one of those TV shows?"

"No, sir. *Dallas Gazette*." She smiled again. "The real news."

His eyes showed a hint of a smile. "You got some ID?"

She fished her driver's license and press pass from her pocket and displayed them in her outstretched hands.

"You like sourdough?"

She could feel her brow furrow at the non sequitur, but she fought it and kept the smile in place. "Who doesn't?"

"You'd be surprised. Everyone wants that newfangled, gluten free, sprouted whatever these days." He turned and started to walk back into the house with the door standing ajar. After a few seconds, he looked back over his shoulder. "You coming? Shut the door behind you. Don't need flies getting in my bread."

The kitchen was a mini-bakery, with fresh-baked loaves of bread lining every surface. The air was thick with the scent of it. Mr. Silver, assuming that was him and not some random stranger, ignored her while he attended to the oven, peering through the window and adjusting the temperature. He was dressed in worn jeans, a button-down white Oxford, and a flour-dusted apron. Her notes said he was sixty years old, but he had the stodgy mannerisms of a man twenty years his elder. Death does that to a person.

"Sit over there," he said, pointing to a chair. "You can talk all you want, but don't mess with the bread."

She complied and watched as he hacked a large slice off one of the cooling loaves, slathered it with soft creamy butter, and dropped the plate in front of her. It rattled for a moment before coming to a stop.

"You want jam? I've got blackberry and peach."

She studied his face for a moment, suspecting his question might be a test. "If it's okay with you, I'll stick with the butter."

He nodded his approval and went back to the oven. She reached for the bread, took a generous bite, and struggled not to moan at the rich, buttery goodness. She'd never had bread this good, and she'd had a lot of bread in her life. She tore into the rest of it and hoped he wouldn't think she was a starving waif stopping by people's doors in hopes of picking up a meal.

"You want another?"

His back was still turned, which kind of freaked her out. Yes, yes, she did want another. She wanted an entire loaf or two and a crock of butter, all to herself, and she wanted to hide away in her house and stuff her face until she couldn't budge, but admitting her weaknesses to a total stranger didn't seem like the way to achieve her goal. A goal that had nothing to do with baked goods. Stop it with the distraction. "It's delicious, but I better not. Thank you."

He turned around and thrust a wrapped bundle onto the table next to her plate. "For later." He wiped his hands on his apron, took it off, and hung it on a hook by the fridge. "Tell me what you want."

The incongruous, nice gesture up against his brisk demeanor threw her for a moment. She wasn't sure what she'd expected. She'd known he would be old, probably a bit broken and sad. But this guy, though definitely older, was spry and peppery and more annoyed than sad. Everyone handled grief differently, and she wasn't about to judge. Sensing he'd respect a direct approach, she didn't shy away. "I want to talk to you about Janelle. About the day she was murdered."

He stiffened slightly, but otherwise his expression didn't change. "There's nothing left to tell."

She got it. He'd probably repeated his story to the police, the press, and anyone else who would listen dozens of times, but she knew from experience there was always one more thing to remember, one detail that would either tie the rest of the facts together or unravel prior assumptions, and she'd keep looking for it no matter who else gave up the fight. "When was the last time you talked to the police?"

He grunted. "They closed her case a long time ago, but I suspect you know that already."

"I do. What if we could get them to reopen it?"

"Oh, so you're one of those optimistic types. And here I took you for a jaded reporter."

She grinned. "I guess you read my work."

"I keep up with the world."

There was a distinct sadness in his voice, like keeping up with the world was a major strain. Again, she got it, but in her case, she couldn't look away from the daily tragedies. She'd made it her life's work. "I want to tell her story."

"You want an exclusive after all these years? You think because her mother is dead now, you'll get your story?"

She didn't want to admit that's exactly what she'd been thinking. After Lauren's murder, her grief had fueled her to focus all her newly acquired reporting skills on the story surrounding the Parks and Rec Killer. She'd had to limit her investigation to her spare time since she'd still been an intern back then, but even with little time to give to the project, she'd managed to alienate some of the grieving relatives, Mrs. Silver included, with her brisk manner and laser focus. She hadn't understood why these people bothered mourning when they could apply that energy into finding the killer. She completely empathized with their pain—a fact she couldn't reveal without disclosing her lack of objectivity—but she couldn't compute why any of them would refuse to talk to her.

Wayne, who'd covered the crime beat back then, had shown up at one of the family's houses to try to get an interview and caught her being ordered off the premises. She'd expected him to be angry, but instead he took her under his tutelage and taught her how to balance persistence with compassion. But it hadn't helped when it came to the Silvers. Beth Silver, Janelle's mother, had been a forceful gatekeeper, and she'd had to wait a long time for this opportunity to speak to Janelle's father alone.

"I want her to receive justice," she said, imparting as much sincerity as she could muster into her voice. He had no reason to believe her. He'd probably been promised justice many times since his daughter's bound and lifeless body had been found years ago, but other than the intrusion of the press, he'd likely received nothing for these empty promises. "I know what it feels like to suffer a huge loss. To feel like the wrong will never be made right."

She waited, hoping she hadn't made a mistake by disclosing her feelings, but she gauged it was worth the risk. If she were here as a caring human instead of an inquisitive reporter, she'd tell him about Lauren, that her curiosity wasn't prurient, but personal because although her friend had been the last, Janelle had been the Parks and Rec Killer's first victim.

He stood and walked back to the stove. Silence thickened the air, but she resisted the urge to dilute it with the sound of her own voice. These were the critical moments when it was important not to press, not to pressure. If he was going to open up to her, it had to be his idea and his alone.

"She was a beautiful girl. Not just pretty, but kind and generous," he said, his voice cracking a bit until he picked up energy. "She wanted to be a vet, although she almost reconsidered at one point because she was worried about having to euthanize animals and she wasn't sure she would be able to do it." He placed another pan in the oven. "Ultimately, she decided it was part of her path—healing and pain were inextricably bound. That's how she was—always able to see the big picture."

"She'd already been accepted to A&M, right?"

"For vet school, yes. She got a lot of teasing from her UT friends about being an Aggie, but there really isn't a better vet school in these parts."

"How did her boyfriend feel about it?" Macy consulted her notes. "David Evans, right?"

He nodded. "He had a hard time with it at first. He thought they'd move back here after graduation and find jobs. Her moving off to College Station for a bunch more school wasn't in his plans, but he eventually came around." His face set in a hard frown. "The police questioned him. Thoroughly."

She'd read the accounts. Of course, David had been the primary suspect, but the police had discarded him as abruptly as they'd latched on. "Do you keep in touch with him?"

"No. He was supposed to be with her that night, but they had a spat. She took off for a run and he went out with his buddies for beer." He bit his bottom lip. "Any other time, it wouldn't have been a big deal, but that night…"

She wanted to avert her eyes in the face of his obvious pain, but witnessing his distress was part of her job no matter how hard it was to see her own suffering reflected there. She remembered the searing pain when she learned Lauren's body had been found mere feet from the jogging trail around White Rock Lake. The burn was as sharp and painful as the day it happened. All she could do now was channel her pain into finding the truth. "How about any of Janelle's other friends from back then. Do you stay in touch with any of them?"

"How about I get to ask a question?" He paused, staring at her as if assessing whether she could handle his inquisition. "Why are you still so interested in Janelle's case after all of this time?"

That was *the* question. The one that had her editor scratching his head and her peers confused. Jerry was the only one who knew she had a personal connection to one of the victims, but even he didn't realize she'd devoted much of her personal life to unearthing clues about the Parks and Rec Killer.

"Let's just say I have a penchant for pursuing stories others have abandoned." She paused, wondering at the wisdom of mentioning her theory. Of all the people she could confide in, this crusty old man seemed like the safest bet to keep her idea under wraps. "The police found a dead body at White Rock Lake last week. It's too soon to tell, but I think it could be related to Janelle's death."

He narrowed his eyes. "Sounds like a coincidence to me."

She kept her expression neutral, not wanting to be too defensive in response to his skepticism. She'd gotten good at that. "Simply stating a fact. Like I said, it's too soon to tell if there's a connection, but it seems worth exploring, don't you think?"

"I gave up on Janelle's killer being found a long time ago." He gestured to the loaves of bread lining his counters. "This is my life. It's simple and easy. The past is the past."

"You're saying you wouldn't want to know the truth if it were possible?"

He looked off into the distance for a moment before answering. "I don't know. Maybe. The truth isn't going to bring her back. It isn't going to make things right."

She knew his response was rational, but it didn't compute. Janelle had been his only child and her life had been ripped away, suddenly and violently. How could he sit here and say that if there was a chance to learn the who and the why behind her murder, he would choose instead to ignore the news and bake bread instead? She wanted to reach across the table, grab him by the shoulders, and shake him until he admitted that, yes, finding Janelle's killer and bringing him to justice was tantamount to moving on.

She balled her fist, digging her nails into her palm, and took a deep breath while she waited for the onslaught of emotion to dissipate. *He's not you. Don't blame the victim. Empathy, not anger.* She played the short phrases on a loop, and the mantra did its trick within a few moments and her breathing started to return to normal.

"Are you okay? You don't look so good."

She met his eyes and forced a smile. "I'm good. I understand why you've put this behind you," she lied, "but my job is to report the news, and if there is a connection behind a recent case and Janelle's that might help catch this scumbag and prevent additional women from suffering a similar fate, I have to pursue it. I'll find out everything I need to on my own, but I had hoped you might help."

His pained expression was a direct result of her stab of guilt, but she was distanced from his pain lest it fuel her own. He stood abruptly. "Come on."

She followed him back through the house toward the front door, and for a moment she considered he might be showing her out, but when they reached the staircase, he started climbing. He was a few steps in when he turned back.

"Are you coming or not?"

"Yes." She placed a hand on the banister and took the steps slowly, sensing where he was leading her was someplace private. Someplace she'd somehow earned the right to see. Fresh bread and secrets—all in an afternoon's work.

He paused before a closed door, and she waited quietly for him to make the next move. "This was her room. When she was a kid. My wife left it exactly the way it was when she went off to college." He turned the knob and pushed the door open, gesturing for her to lead the way. Macy walked across the threshold, slow steps to allow her to take in the time capsule of Janelle's bedroom.

Posters featuring Destiny's Child and the Black Eyed Peas lined the wall along with a bunch of certificates from the National Honor Society. She swept her gaze over every surface and marveled at the time capsule feel of the entire room. Any minute, Janelle would walk through the door and resume her life as if nothing had happened.

"It's like a shrine, I know."

She turned to face him. "Did the police search here?"

He hunched his shoulders. "No need. She didn't live here at the time. This is all stuff she left when she moved out." He pointed to a desk in the corner. "There are a few things over there that we saved from her apartment. Some outfit that does estate sales sold off the furniture and clothes. We couldn't deal with it at the time."

Judging by the way this room looked, he probably still couldn't deal with it. Her spine tingled as she realized if she found anything here, anything helpful to the case, she might be the one seeing it for the very first time. She pointed at the desk. "May I?"

"Help yourself. She kept an address book and some journals. In the first drawer." He edged toward the door. "Bread's about to come out of the oven. Stay as long as you want."

She barely noticed his exit. The cushion on the chair was worn and flat, but the discomfort was small compared to the veritable treasure trove of information that existed in this space. The address book was exactly where he'd said it would be and next to it were four thin leather journals—one for each year of high school. Doubtful they would provide any direct information about her killer, but they were likely to contain valuable background information about her desires, her habits, her relationships—all details that might shed light on any vulnerabilities she might possess that the killer had taken advantage of.

She snapped twenty-six photos—one for every page in the address book, and then settled in to read.

CHAPTER SEVEN

Beck pulled into the parking lot and sat for a few minutes as if by pressing pause, she could revert back to the life she'd had a few months ago. After a few minutes of sitting in the silence with only the voices in her head telling her she'd fucked up royally, she decided it would be better to go inside and face her punishment than continue this self-flagellation.

She'd worked out of the White Rock substation since she'd started on the force, only showing up at headquarters for commendation ceremonies and the occasional meeting with the higher-ups. She'd expected she might be transferred to another station after she'd made detective, but this outpost in South Dallas had never figured into her equation. But the cold case unit was located within the walls of this old, off-the-beaten-path building, so this was her new home until she figured out how to get back to the job. The real job.

Unlike the other stations she'd been to, this one didn't have much in the way of security. The duty officer at the front desk was a youngster with a crew cut whose badge read Officer Foster. She strode over and announced, "I'm here to see Sergeant Mendoza."

"Name?"

She wasn't sure if he was joking since her picture had been plastered all over the news, but he had an I'm really serious look about him, so she simply said, "Ramsey."

He pointed to a short row of chairs. "Have a seat."

A few minutes later, a short, stocky woman burst out of the office door behind the gatekeeper. "Do not put that man through to me again," she said to Foster. "There's only so many ways I can tell him I know nothing."

"Yes, ma'am." Foster pointed at Beck. "Ramsey's here."

The woman looked her up and down, and Beck didn't get a good feel for whether she passed the appraisal. Finally, the woman stuck out her hand. "Sergeant Mendoza. Come with me."

Beck returned the strong grip and followed Mendoza into her office. It was a tight fit, which told her a lot about how cold cases ranked. About what she'd figured.

"Sit," Mendoza said and then did the same. "So, looks like we're stuck with each other. I know what you did to pull this assignment." She pointed at her chest. "Me? I don't want to be here either, but I'm not here because I ratted out my partner. Now we know something about each other and that's all the small talk we need to exchange. Understood?"

"Sure." Beck was ambivalent. She hadn't expected to make new friends, but other than that she didn't know what to expect. The cold case squad was anathema. TV shows made it seem like it would be bustling with detectives working diligently to dig up new facts guaranteed to land them a cameo in primetime, but among fellow cops, it was known as a dungeon where careers went to die. She hoped it was merely purgatory, and when she'd done her penance, she'd be free to get back to real work.

"Come on, I'll show you to your desk."

She followed Mendoza down a long hallway to the door at the end. Mendoza held the door open, and she walked through into a maze of boxes. She stood still for a moment, a little overwhelmed by the cardboard city that was her new home.

"Don't worry about it," Mendoza said. "You won't even look at most of these." She pointed to a small desk in the right corner. "That's for you. Password to the computer is on a Post-it in the desk drawer, and instructions are there too. There's some pens and pads of paper in the desk. You shouldn't need anything else. Cell signal in here sucks, so if you want to make a call, you'll probably need to go outside. Hours are eight to five. Take your meal break whenever you want. I'm going back to my office. Have fun."

Mendoza was about to shut the door behind her when she thought to ask. "What do you want me to do?"

"Do?" Mendoza grunted. "There's not much to be done. These cases are unsolvable. You know the drill—if there aren't any clear leads in the first week, chances are slim there ever will be. This squad is the brainchild of the mayor because he loves all that TV crap about true crime, and we're here to appease him. Comb through the files, make lists, whatever makes you happy, but all I need is for you to finish filling out the case log. It's on the computer. Just start where the last person left off."

The last person. How many other people had funneled through this space on their way back to redemption, and how long a sentence was the norm? She had no idea and focusing on it would only drive her crazy. Time to do her time and be grateful she'd be doing it in peace.

An hour later, she was yawning, and her eyes were blurry, and she was no longer grateful for anything about being stuck alone in this godforsaken place. And she wasn't even a quarter of the way through the first box. Coffee. That's what she needed. She walked back to the front of the office. Foster was on the phone, so she looked around but didn't find any sign of a coffee maker or any other creature comforts.

"What are you looking for?"

She turned at the sound of his voice. His tone was neutral, and she couldn't get a read on whether he harbored the same level of hostility as the rest of the force had against her, but at this point she was becoming immune to it. "Coffee."

He raised a thermos. "Home brew. We don't have a machine." He unscrewed the top of this thermos. "You want some? My wife makes it special for me."

Surprised at the generous offer, she decided she had to accept. Other than Mendoza, he was the first fellow cop who'd spoken to her voluntarily since Jack had been arrested. "I'd love some, but I don't have a mug."

He unscrewed the cup off the thermos, poured it full of delicious smelling coffee, and handed it to her. "Don't have any condiments."

She raised the cup to her lips and took a sip. "Don't need any with coffee this good. Your wife must love you."

He cracked a grin. "Yeah, I think so."

"What did you do to get stuck here?"

He rolled his chair back and pointed at the cast on his leg. "Fell off a damn fence while in pursuit. Not only did I break my leg, but I got bit by a damn dog."

"Ouch. Hope you caught the perp."

He nodded. "I fell right on top of the bony bastard, which probably didn't help the whole leg situation."

"Prognosis?"

"My next PT check in is in two weeks and I'll find out then if I can get back on the street. I hear I'm getting assigned to the White Rock subdivision."

"Some good people there," she said, wondering if any of those good people would say the same about her anymore. It wasn't like any of her old buddies were reaching out these days. "I guess you know why I'm here."

"You turned in your partner."

"I told the truth about what happened."

"Different explanation, same result."

He was right, but she wanted to protest, explain her actions, but it was pointless. No one seemed interested in the distinction. It wasn't like Jack had done something in secret and she'd had a choice not to speak up. A real person had been gunned down with real bullets. Aldridge was dead now and everyone knew Jack did it. She'd told the truth about what she'd seen, and Jack had put her in that position by not turning on his body cam or the car cam.

What happened to him next was up to the grand jury, the DA, a judge, and jury. All she'd done was report the truth when she was questioned about it. She'd expect no less from Jack if their roles were reversed.

But if their roles were reversed, this never would've happened. If she'd been the one driving, she wouldn't have made the stop in the first place under such bogus pretenses.

So why had Jack?

She'd gone over the last few months in her head many times, looking for signs he'd been crossing the line, and in retrospect, she could see some. He'd become increasingly belligerent with suspects, quick to anger. But nothing she'd identified at the time as a direct line to abuse of force, and certainly nothing actionable. She'd spent more time with him than anyone else other than his wife, and sometimes more than her. How was it possible she hadn't seen this coming?

She turned back to Foster who'd resumed whatever he was doing between sips of coffee. As if he could feel her gaze, he looked up and met her eyes.

"Something on your mind?"

"Maybe I'm curious about why you're talking to me when everyone else thinks I have the plague."

"They don't think you have the plague. They're all thinking 'shit, that could've been me.'"

"Who? Me or Jack?"

He shrugged. "Either. Jack for the ones that cross the line and you for the ones that have seen it but never reported it. You make the first set scared and the second set guilty."

"Which side are you on?"

"Sides are for dodgeball. Life's too complicated to divvy things up that way. You did what you felt you had to do and what happens next isn't up to me or you or your partner."

"They teach you to be a wise sage in the service?"

He cocked his head, his expression curious. "How'd you know?"

"Lucky guess," she said, pleased her instincts were still intact. "My brother did a couple of tours. You guys all have a few distinctive tells."

"Hmm." He jerked his chin to the back room. "Mendoza will be back soon. Just a warning—she's not a fan of folks standing around. Assistant chief's been on her to get that log done, and the wrath flows downhill if you get me."

She got him, loud and clear. Back to the busy work. The encouraging thing about his comment was that despite Mendoza's apparent disdain for these cold cases, perhaps the higher-ups really did care about solving them, and the idea of working on something that mattered motivated her to get back to it.

She finished her coffee and set the cup on his desk. She wanted to say something else. Something about how she was grateful he'd spoken to her and not to hurl a threat or merely call her a fucking bitch, but she sensed acknowledging the power imbalance would only make them both uncomfortable. With a simple, "see you later" she turned to the room full of boxes and resumed her miserable clerical work, wishing her troubles could heal as tangibly as Foster's leg.

CHAPTER EIGHT

Macy was two steps from her office door when she heard Jerry's voice calling her name. She was tempted to keep walking, but his tone carried the kind of urgency she only heard when he was in crisis mode. "Hey, Jerry."

He pointed at her office door. "We need to talk."

The "we" implied she was gripped by the same need. "I was hoping to get a few minutes alone. I was finally able to interview Janelle Silver's father, and I want to organize my notes for the first installment of the feature."

"That's what we need to talk about." He pointed again. "Come on."

Resigned, she opened the door, led the way inside, and sat at her desk. Jerry shut the door behind them, but remained standing, his expression serious. She pointed at the chair across from her. "Sit down. You're making me nervous looming over me."

"This won't take long. The board of directors held a meeting this morning."

"And?"

"And there's going to be some big changes."

The dribble of information made her nervous. "They've already been making changes."

"Bigger ones."

His ominous tone and the fact he wasn't simply telling her straightaway what the changes would be signaled the news was bad. Very bad. Her stomach turned and she braced for whatever he had to say. "Okay, I assume whatever happened affects me personally or you wouldn't have shown up at my door with your grim reaper face. Spill it."

"They ordered us to focus on syndicated content. Big national names and AP news feeds. Scaled down metro section and limited space for anything that isn't national news."

"So, basically they want to print only what any moron can find online for free?" Now she was angry. "Great business model."

He cleared his throat. "You're going to have to drop your feature."

His words struck her like a hammer. "You're kidding."

"I'm not. I'm not going to have space to run it and I can't justify resurrecting a ten-year-old case when I'm barely going to have room to run breaking news."

"Cases."

"What?"

"You said 'case,' but there's more than one. For God's sake, I'm talking about a serial killer who might still be roaming the streets."

"Tell me what hard evidence you have that the Parks and Rec Killer is back in action. Do you have a statement from a detective currently working leads? A statement from anyone in law enforcement at all?"

"Not yet. I'm working on it, but Jerry, I saw the body with my own eyes, and I don't need some detective to tell me what I saw. It's the same M.O. Besides, law enforcement has a vested interest in not connecting the cases because it points out their ineptitude for not catching the killer in the first place." She placed both hands on the desk and stared at him, trying to read his intent. "I shouldn't have to tell you that."

He glanced back at the closed door and leaned closer. "And I shouldn't have to tell you that I'm doing everything I can to keep us all employed. You think these people care about quality news? All they care about is selling ad revenue with whatever flash in the pan sound bite is trending in the moment. It's taking everything I have to keep them from chopping us up and selling us to the highest bidder, and you know the result will be even worse. The days when you could spend months investigating a piece are gone—here at least. If we're not producing printable copy, guaranteed to go viral, or whatever, then they have no use for us." He held up his hand, thumb and forefinger less than an inch apart. "They are this close to gutting our staff and replacing us with a bunch of interns who can repost whatever comes in off the wire and churn out clickbait columns they stole from social media. Please don't fight me on this."

She'd been fighting him for years, but never in a truly acrimonious way. Their sparring was mostly about expenses and deadlines, but she'd never genuinely pushed him beyond what she knew was possible, and he'd never pushed back when she'd dug in her heels about a story. His worried eyes told her this time was different. His sense of foreboding was strong, but how could she give up now?

"Is there any way to make this work?" she asked. "This story is important, and not just to me."

"I need something that will sell like hotcakes. You bring me a banner headline, and I'll go to bat for you on the feature piece."

"Like what?"

"Get an exclusive interview with Beck Ramsey."

Macy flashed back to her encounter with the gorgeous woman at the hearing a few weeks ago. "Officer Ramsey? She's not going to do a sit-down. Not while the case is pending."

"Grand jury's already reported out and her reputation has been smeared all over. What does she have to lose? Besides, it's *Detective* Ramsey now. Can you believe it? They promoted her and then sidelined her in the same cruel swipe. If they try to silence her now, they'll come across looking like idiots."

"Detective? They seriously have her going out and investigating cases?"

"Word is she's been relegated to the cold case squad. I'm sure it's so they can keep her tucked away from the public eye. She's got to be itching to talk to someone by now and give her side of the story."

Macy heard "cold case" and the rest of Jerry's words blurred. Her mind started churning, but there was only one possible conclusion. "I'll do it."

"Excuse me?"

"Don't act so surprised. I'll do it, but you have to promise you'll get the board to back off when it comes to the feature."

"You get Beck Ramsey to give you a sit-down exclusive and I'll give it everything I've got."

"You got it." She shooed him out of the room. "Now go, so I can work my magic." She waited until he cleared the door before she put her head on her desk and allowed herself a moment to decompress. She needed to get an interview with Ramsey, and she needed to speed up her work on the Parks and Rec case, both about the past case and what might be developing now. She'd already left several messages for Detective Claire Hanlon about the body that had been found by White Rock Lake, but Claire hadn't had much intel to share that hadn't already made it into the public domain. Yes, this victim had been bound and strangled, like the Parks and Rec Killer, but unlike the cases from ten years ago, the killer's handiwork was disorganized, and there'd been signs of a struggle. Claire was waiting on a report from the ME about whether any viable DNA had been recovered, and Macy made a mental note to follow up with her about that.

But right now, she had to figure out a way to get everything done so she could keep her feature piece. At that moment, Wayne's face popped in her head along with memories of showing up at his office door with his favorite donuts whenever she needed advice about a story. Maybe running into him was a fortuitous event. Before she could give it more thought, she picked up the phone and dialed his number.

"Paxton here."

"Hey, Wayne. It's Macy. Bet you didn't expect to hear from me so soon. You free for lunch?"

After a slight pause, he replied, "Sure. What time?"

"How about right now?"

"It's barely ten a.m. Too early for Louie's."

"It's noon somewhere. Pretend it's brunch."

"Fine, but you're buying. Market Diner in thirty minutes. See you there."

She smiled as she clicked off the line. They'd shared many a breakfast at the Dallas mainstay. He'd introduced her to the place, but she'd stopped going nearly as much after he moved away.

She made great time, and in twenty minutes, she walked through the diner doors, surprised to see Wayne already waiting for her at a corner booth. She smiled at the hostess with the beehive hairdo and slid into the booth across from him. "Somebody made good time. I thought you said you were living up north these days."

"I am, but I was running some errands off I-35, which made your call perfectly timed."

She started to look at the menu, but he pulled it out of her hand. "Don't bother. I already ordered for you."

"Really? What are we having?"

"Two eggs, over easy. Wheat toast, grits, and bacon. Extra crisp."

"I'm impressed at your memory, but what if I've gone vegan?"

"Then I hope you enjoy the toast and grits. Better tell the waitress no butter."

"As if. Butter is one of the reasons I get up in the morning." Macy patted her stomach and vowed she would try and get to the gym this week—a vow she was likely to break. She had several more interviews to get for the feature piece, not to mention trying to convince Beck Ramsey to talk to her, which brought her back to the reason she'd called Wayne in the first place. "I need some advice."

"You sure I'm the right person to ask? I haven't worked a beat since I moved to New Jersey."

"That must've been hard on you." He'd taken an early retirement and moved to be closer to his in-laws at his wife

Cathy's request after what had seemed like a manageable cancer diagnosis had taken a turn for the worse. She'd kept in touch with him at first—sending notes of encouragement and updates on the local news and politics at the paper, but like most long-distance relationships, their communication had waned. He'd been busy dealing with a wife in decline and she'd been focused on her career. She was embarrassed at the realization it had been several years since she'd last corresponded with him.

"It was," he said. "Cathy rallied over and over, but every time was followed by another decline. I worked some freelance gigs, but there's no way I could've held down a full-time job." He sighed and wiped the corner of his eyes. "I'm grateful I was able to be at her side all that time, but it took its toll. I want to jump back in, but the news game has changed a lot in the past eight years. Hell, it's changed in the past year. I don't know how you keep up."

The waitress showed up with their food before she could answer, and they spent the next few minutes eating. As Macy shoveled food in her mouth, she realized she'd forgotten to eat before she left the house that morning, an event that had been all too common since she'd delved back into her research on the Parks and Rec Killer.

"It's not easy," she said. "All anyone seems to care about is clickbait. Subscriptions are almost nonexistent, so ad sales are where it's at. Whatever can drive people to buy shit they don't need. That's for sure all the board is focused on these days. And don't even get me started about shelf-life. It's been getting bad for a while, but the rate at which news goes stale is next-level crazy. I'm having to fight to do any feature length pieces, which brings me back to the advice segment of our meal."

He set his fork down and stared directly at her. "Shoot."

"I've been working on a feature spread about the Parks and Rec Killer. It's been ten years since the anniversary of Lauren's death."

He shook his head. "I remember. It was hard on you. On all of us."

She reached for his hand and squeezed it. "I don't know how I would've made it without you. 'Focus on the facts not your feelings.' I remember you saying that like it was yesterday. Which is why I decided to write this piece." She took a deep breath. "He's still out there and I cannot tell you how much that gets under my skin. I think about it every day."

"Of course you do."

"My friends say I'm obsessed. That I should stop working on this piece and put it behind me once and for all."

"And you want my opinion? Is that why you asked me here today?"

"Partly. Jerry wants to drop the piece, but he says he'll go to bat for me with the board if I get an interview he wants about a police involved shooting."

"Staples, right?"

She smiled. "I should've known you'd be up on the local news. Yes, Jerry wants me to get an exclusive from his partner, Beck Ramsey."

"Can you?"

"Do you even know me? Of course, I can. And the bonus is, she's working cold cases right now."

He nodded slowly. "I see where you're going with this. Give her a slant on the interview in exchange for some access."

"That's pretty much it. Feels a little smarmy."

"It's only smarmy if you let it be. Tell her the truth. You'll listen to everything she has to say and print the truth, but the whole truth. Tell her it's the rest of the press, Jack's lawyer, and the public who will slant the story, but if she talks to you, you will be fair and impartial. You won't hold back on the questions you ask, but you'll print the full answer—no editing to get flash over substance. And make Jerry promise in advance that he'll run the whole damn thing."

"You make it sound so easy."

"Damn, girl, you were in the running for a Pulitzer. You have to leverage that for as long as you can." He smiled. "And as for your friends, family, or whoever else tells you that being obsessed about a story is a bad thing. Screw 'em. The story is the thing. What you do is as important as anything else out there. Don't let anyone or anything get in your way."

An hour later, back at the office, Macy replayed his words. *The story is the thing.* It was the premise she'd lived by since she'd started with the paper. Her dedication to her work had cost her a personal life and she'd never minded because the story was the thing. Every story, not just this one, but if she could find a way to end this tale with some real closure, maybe, just maybe, the story wouldn't have to be the only thing in her life.

Until then, she had work to do.

At exactly five o'clock, Beck walked out of the substation and, after spending an entire day locked away in the dead file room, blinked to adjust to the light of the full summer sun. She supposed she should be grateful to work in the air-conditioned setting since on a usual day, she'd be fighting with Jack over the AC control on the dash of their patrol car. Except she was never going to be on patrol again and never be working with Jack either. She was a detective now, but relegated to cases no one cared about, working solo, sequestered from the family who she'd thought would have her back, no matter what. The betrayal and Mendoza's clear message that she was to simply log the files but not look at the contents was the reason she'd left at five straight up. No sense trying to impress anyone with her work ethic here. There was no one to impress and no one cared.

But after a day in solitary slogging through data entry, now she was craving company. She pulled out her phone to text Liam to see if he had plans, when she heard a voice call her name. She turned at the sound, startled to see the reporter who'd followed her out of the building after the hearing on Jack's case standing a few feet away. Macy something. What was she doing here, but more importantly, how had she managed to get so close without her noticing? Apparently, working in a file room was causing her to lose her edge.

"I told you no comment before and that hasn't changed." She called out the words, hoping they would deter Macy from pressing her for an interview.

The woman flashed a smile—one that probably worked with a lot of other targets of her nosy ways. "How about I do the talking? You can listen, and if you feel like chiming in, you can." She raised her hands in mock surrender. "No pressure."

Beck glanced around the parking lot. Foster had left early for a PT appointment and Mendoza was hardly ever around, today being no exception. "Fine. Start talking."

Macy nodded. "I think you got the raw end of this deal."

"That's not how you wrote your last story."

"I work with the information I have in the moment."

"And then you stalk your victims until they give in?"

"I'm not stalking you, but I would like to hear your side."

"Because it will sell papers?"

"Sure, but also because I think it's important to tell the whole story. Look me up. I'm known for offering perspective. You don't have to take my word for it." Macy backed away a few steps, hands raised in surrender. "Tell you what. Why don't I leave now and let you do that? I have an errand to run and then I'm headed to JR's for a beer. Join me there in about thirty minutes, and I'll buy the first round and give you my full rundown. I'll wait an hour and if you don't show up, I promise I won't bother you again."

"So, if I don't show up, you'll drop the story?"

"Hell no." Macy grinned. "This is a big case and it's going to get lots of coverage. If you choose not to talk to me, I'll write the story with the info I've got. I'd like to include your take, but if it's 'no comment' then that's what it is." She jingled her keys in the air. "If you get there soon, I'll even buy you a burger."

She turned and walked to her car and gave a friendly wave before she drove away. Beck had to force herself not to return the good-bye, but she did watch Macy's car until it disappeared from sight. The moment they'd parted, she'd been steadfast she wasn't about to take Macy up on her offer, but with each passing moment, the earnestness she'd seen in Macy's expression lured her into thinking perhaps she could trust her.

She climbed into her Jeep and started the engine to get the AC going. While she waited for it to cool down, she pulled out her phone and googled Macy's name. The first few entries were nothing surprising. The local paper was fond of touting Macy's Pulitzer nod for investigative reporting. The milestone was several years old and though she'd finaled, she hadn't gone on to win. She read further to determine the type of story that had been deemed award worthy. Illegal dumping. Nothing seedy or prurient designed to sell papers rather than serve the readership. Mark one in the pro-Macy column.

Wait. Was she really considering meeting with a reporter to talk about Jack's case? Her union rep would come unhinged if he knew she was even thinking about it, let alone leaning in that direction. While one part of her was imagining his face, red and swelling with agitation, the rest of her mental screen filled with an image of Macy standing in the parking lot, waiting for her as she exited the station. Macy was hot, and normally a woman who exuded her kind of unapologetic self-confidence would be a big draw.

Beck shook her head. If she wasn't caught up in Jack's mess, if she was a real detective instead of a glorified data entry clerk, and she didn't know Macy was a reporter, she might've flirted a little, handed over her number, made an effort to impress. But her predicament took that option off the table. Completely.

Which brought her back around to the idea that possibly talking to Macy in her role as reporter might be a good idea. She could explain why she did what she did that night and why she didn't do what she didn't do. Even as she heard the thought in her head, she wasn't sure she could explain the latter. If she had it to do all over, she liked to think she would've tackled Jack and wrestled him to the ground to keep him from shooting Aldridge. But hindsight was a precarious thing, allowing the viewer to make leisurely decisions in slow-motion about how they would've reacted when events unfolding in real time happened too quickly and under too much stress and rarely allowed in-the-moment reflection. How could a reporter get that without ever having been placed in the same position?

She pulled out of the parking lot and drove north, telling herself she didn't have to decide right now. She had an hour. Less if she wanted a burger. Macy's eager expression, urging her to tell her side and promising an impartial listener, flashed in her memory. A burger was the last thing on her mind right now, which told her all she needed to know.

Chapter Nine

Macy took the ice-cold mug from Dawson, her favorite bartender at J.R.'s, and immediately took a drink, savoring the crisp, cool tang of the IPA against the heat of the day. It was the last week in June and it was already sweltering, which didn't bode well for the rest of the summer. Thank God for bars with cold beer on tap and heavy-duty air conditioning.

On his next pass by, Dawson asked if she wanted to order any food. Not surprising since she'd been grabbing dinner here a couple of nights a week for as long as she could remember. By herself, on a barstool, with the game on the TV and Dawson or whoever else was on duty ready to serve as a built-in family. Harrison had often teased her about her choice to hang out at the guys' bar when the popular women's bar, Sue Ellen's, was right around the corner. But here she never had to worry about whether someone was talking to her because they were being nice or if they wanted something more. It was easier to be here than to explain she already had enough on her plate without adding dating to the mix.

She glanced toward the door. She'd told Beck she'd wait an hour, but it was going to be a long sixty minutes if she spent the entire time wondering if Beck would take her up on the invitation. *It wasn't like you were exactly pleasant when you asked her to join you.*

True. Her gruff approach might not have been the best way to get Beck to talk to her. Her mind wandered to other ways she could coax Beck into giving her an interview. She needed this win if she wanted to stave off the bean counters from shutting down the last vestiges of real reporting at the paper. If Beck would only do her part by showing up, she was certain she could get her to talk, to tell her side of the story which she hadn't shared with anyone firsthand other than the police. Macy picked up her phone. She'd managed to get Beck's number from one of her sources in the department. Maybe she could be nice and more cajoling in a text.

She was three words in when she heard a familiar voice over her shoulder.

"If you think I still have that phone number, you're not as good a reporter as the internet says you are."

Without missing a beat, Macy turned to face Beck. "I'm not sure whether to be impressed you looked me up or insulted you didn't know anything about me in the first place."

"Let's just say I don't always trust what I hear. I like to do my own research." Beck pointed at the seat next to Macy, and at her nod, sat down, but didn't relax into the seat. Macy sensed that she was like a skittish colt—one wrong move and she was out of here. Knowing that, she didn't press and did her best to hide her impatience.

Dawson strode over and set a coaster in front of Beck. "What'll it be?"

"Beck, meet my favorite bartender, Dawson."

Beck nodded at Dawson and glanced over at Macy's mug. "Jameson's. Neat."

Macy took note of the preference, wanting to remark about the choice of hard liquor, but holding her tongue. She waited until Dawson had finished his pour and set a glass in front of Beck before speaking. "And what did your research tell you?"

Beck picked up the glass and sipped the whiskey, her eyes fluttering shut for a moment before she sighed and set the glass back down. "You used to cover the metro desk, but now you mostly write feature stories. You've been short-listed for a Pulitzer, but you didn't win, and word is you never will because you don't play politics with the powers that be. You have a lot of sources on the force, but no one knows who they are, which I suppose means you're good at keeping secrets, which is kind of ironic considering your job is to tell the news."

Macy nodded in respect at the succinct summary of her career. "That was pretty good. Shall I take a turn?"

Beck raised her glass and tilted it toward her. "Go for it."

"You were a rising star, on track to becoming detective when your partner gunned down a suspect for no reason. You told the truth and now you're paying for it with a stint on the cold case squad. You made detective, but it'll be hard to use your shield for anything meaningful when you're stuck in a warehouse reviewing files no one cares about. I'm thinking right about now you're reconsidering your career decision and looking for a way out, but you've got cop in your blood and you're not likely to abandon your calling without a lot of consideration."

"Not bad. But who says no one cares about the cold cases?"

"How many are you actively investigating right now?" She watched Beck's face and caught her adjusting her expression. "You don't have to give me real numbers. I'm not writing an exclusive on the subject, but Mendoza isn't one for digging deep."

"Sounds like you've been doing some digging of your own."

"I do have an interest in a particular set of cold cases." She stopped short while she decided whether to split her focus. Better to wait until she'd developed some kind of relationship before proposing the quid pro quo. "But I asked you here to talk about your case."

"It's not my case. It's Staples's case. I'm just a witness."

"The star witness."

"I'm no star."

"Next you're going to say, 'just doing my job, ma'am.'"

"You don't look like you'd enjoy being called ma'am."

"I'm not quite sure how to take that." Macy took a drink from her beer while she considered the fact she wasn't quite sure of a lot of things when it came to Beck Ramsey. Normally, she'd hard charge into this story, content to publish a litany of "no comments" if she didn't get the answer to pointed questions, but there was a lot more to this if she wanted to work Beck as a potential source. The trick was getting the story Jerry wanted and getting the information she needed for her feature piece and balancing both without losing her integrity in the process. Thankfully, Dawson appeared before she had to take the next step.

"You two hungry?" he asked, casting her a sly side glance.

Macy answered quickly to deflect his implication. "I am. Detective?"

Beck looked visibly startled at the moniker. "It's Beck and yeah, I could eat."

"Looks like it's two burgers, Dawson." She turned to Beck. "The works?"

"Of course."

Macy liked her already. "Great." She shot Dawson a pointed look. "We're all set for now." She waited until he'd wandered to the far side of the bar before resuming her conversation with Beck. "Staples fired his other lawyer and hired Gloria Leland to defend him."

"I hadn't heard."

"You seem unfazed."

"If you'd been through what I've been through over the past month, you'd be unfazed too."

"I'd be interested in hearing about it."

"For your article? No, thanks. I already had to spill my guts to a department therapist. I don't need to see my feelings splashed across the front page."

Macy grinned. "Ah, so you have front-page-worthy feelings. Good to know."

Beck pointed at her face. "See. This is exactly why I have no interest in talking about anything outside of the statement I've already given."

Then why did you agree to meet me at all? Macy filed away the question to examine later. Right now, her only focus was to get Beck talking. "Seriously though, I am interested in how you feel about what happened and how you were treated afterward. We can do this part off the record."

"Why would you agree to that?"

"Off the record?" Macy chose her words carefully. "Because anything you tell me can provide context. I don't need to use it all to write a compelling story." Partly true. In a normal situation, she wouldn't want to declare anything off limits, but this wasn't normal. For one thing, she didn't want to do this story in the first place, so other than the potential for developing Beck as a source, she was here to move through the paces to please her editor long enough to get her feature up and running. "If you want more time to check me out, I can put this article off for a bit, but not long."

She watched Beck carefully and caught a glimpse of angst before her features settled into a neutral, just the facts, ma'am, expression. The glimpse gave her hope. Beck was still sensitive to what people thought about her, which might give her motivation to share her side of the story and might even motivate her to actually want to work some of the cold cases on her desk no matter how hard Mendoza worked to keep them buried.

Dawson showed up with their burgers and they both dug in. After a few moments of hunger-satisfying silence, their conversation turned to other things: the weather, development in the neighborhood, and the upcoming city council runoff. Macy made a snap judgment about how comfortable Beck seemed sitting in a gay bar and decided to venture a question to satisfy her personal curiosity. "I guess you won't be working Pride this year since you've been promoted."

A flicker of surprise at the question was quickly replaced by a nod. "Probably for the best. I have a feeling my presence would be a distraction."

"If you were in uniform, sure. But now you're free to show up in shorts and a tank top and mingle with the masses. You're one rainbow hat away from being incognito."

Beck shrugged. "I guess."

"You've never been before, have you? I mean just for fun."

"No. I mean, I've always taken the work shift that day. I figured my place was making sure cops assigned were actually family instead of gawkers. No tank tops and shorts for me."

Macy spent a few seconds imagining Beck's bare shoulders and legs, and it was difficult to snap back to pretending all she wanted was Beck's side of the Jack Staples story. "Too bad," she murmured.

"What's that?"

Macy shook her head like it was a snow globe transforming the image. "Nothing. But whatever you wear, you should go for fun at least once in your life."

"You don't strike me as the kind of person who's an authority on fun."

"Is that so? I'm trying to figure out if that's a compliment or a dig."

"Neither. Simply stating an observation. You're…" Beck paused and stared at the ceiling like the answer would descend into her brain. "Intense."

The word stung, probably because Jerry had used it several times this week, and the week before that, it had been her best friends who'd slung around the adjective, referencing her lack of time to get together with them while she was obsessed with this story. None of them meant it as a compliment. Rather, it was a word designed to signal whatever she did or said should be viewed through a lens of suspicion—that she should be subject to greater scrutiny because her perspective was off.

But it wasn't. Her intensity was the reason she was first to uncover the truth, right the wrongs, avenge evil.

Oh, okay, so maybe she was a little intense, but with good reason. The one truth that had eluded her so far meant she'd remain that way. For now, anyway. She looked over at Beck who was studying her…intensely—there really wasn't any other word for it—and it occurred to her she and Beck had basically the same job duties. Interview principals and witnesses regarding an event. Observe and gather evidence. Summarize the details into a report and publish it for anyone who wanted to read it. The differences stopped there, but there were enough of them to give her a feeling of kinship when it came to Beck and an idea for how they could both get what they wanted. "I have an idea."

❖

Beck took another sip from her whiskey to burn away the dread while she waited for Macy to explain her idea. A beer would have been a better choice with the burger, but lately she'd craved or rather needed stronger medicine to stave off the constant barrage of her daily life, and whatever Macy was about to say probably merited a double. "Let's hear it."

"You're getting trashed in the press. Let me do a profile piece. We don't even have to talk about the facts of what happened that night. I'll focus on you, your relationship with Staples, then and now, and how being at the center of this storm has affected your life. You toss me a few background tidbits no one else knows, and my editor will be satisfied, and we'll back off."

Beck studied her for a moment, sensing there was a catch. "What do you get out of it?"

"Besides an exclusive with you?" Macy pushed her food around her plate, not making eye contact. "I'm working on a piece about an old case." She looked up and met Beck's stare. "A cold case."

Ah, so that was it. "And you want a look at some files."

"Yes."

"You don't need me for that. File a FOIA request."

Macy bit her bottom lip. "I have. They tend to get bogged down."

Beck nodded. She'd come across a stack of them at the office, shoved in a box situated well behind the others. She'd asked Mendoza about them only to be told they were being handled, which she believed to be a lie, but she had no reason to care one way or the other. "There are channels."

"Yes, there are." Macy fixed her with a stare. "And I'm exploring one of them right now."

Beck set down her glass and pushed away from the bar. "I'm not a channel for you to explore. To exploit." A second later, Macy's hand was on her arm, and she instantly warmed to the firm yet gentle touch, surprised by her own reaction.

"I'm not trying to exploit you," Macy said. "I guess I assumed you were the kind of person who thought the truth was more important than traditions. You know, traditions like stalling reporters and hiding the illegal actions of fellow officers."

And just like that Macy had perfectly summed up her personal dilemma. She *was* that kind of person, but she'd always thought being that way meant she would rise above, but she'd never felt as buried under as she did right now. Her career was essentially over, and she'd lost all her friends. Some might say neither one of those things was worth very much if they were so easy to lose, but when you dedicated your life to something, shouldn't you get to reap the rewards of your hard work?

Which begged the question of whether talking to Macy about it would improve her current circumstance or only make things worse. All she knew in this moment was that she didn't know, and she shouldn't make any snap decisions. "I'll think about it." At Macy's intense gaze, she added, "It's the best I can do."

Macy held out her hand. "Give me your phone."

"What?"

"You heard me." Macy waved her outstretched phone. "Come on."

Beck picked her phone up off the bar, stared at the screen to unlock it, and handed it to Macy, praying she wasn't making a huge mistake. What kind of cop handed their phone over to a virtual stranger? Or worst yet, a reporter. She watched Macy's deliberate keystrokes, slightly mesmerized by her massive self-confidence and control of the situation. Normally, she'd find it sexy, but this wasn't normal, and she had no business treating this meeting like anything other than a business arrangement.

"Here you go." Macy shoved the phone at her.

"I assume you gave me your number."

"And a deadline." Macy pointed at the now locked screen. "Sunday. Cedar Springs." She waved at the bartender and motioned for him to bring the check while she slid out of her seat. "I'll meet you right out front."

While Beck digested the fact Macy was trying to trick her into attending Pride, Dawson brought the check and Macy signed the credit card form, waving off her protest. Macy stuffed the receipt in her pocket. "See you Sunday," she said as she headed to the door.

"Wait," Beck called out, acutely conscious about how much she wanted Macy to stick around. "What if I don't show?"

"Then I guess I have my answer."

Her stare burned a hole in Beck's resolve, and she hoped it didn't show. She may as well have been wishing for a unicorn.

"But I hope you will." Macy smiled, a rich, full, genuine smile. "I think you will."

She turned away and walked to the door, and Beck watched her exit, kind of hoping Macy would look back one last time, but unsure what she would do if she did.

"She's kind of a whirlwind, right?"

She looked up to see Dawson standing across from her. "I guess. I don't really know her."

"You'll find out soon enough." He wiped down the bar top in front of where Macy had been sitting. "She's good people though."

"Okay." She made a show of pulling up her phone to avoid further chitchat since her instincts told her that this conversation would give him more intel than she could hope to get in return.

"You want another drink?"

She stared at her empty glass with a fond recollection of the pleasant burn. Yes, she definitely would like another. And another. And another. But that much whiskey led to trouble, and she didn't need more. But she also didn't want to leave this cocoon where no one seemed to recognize her and point and stare. "I'll have a draft. Something light."

Dawson nodded and headed to the tap at the other end of the bar. While he was pouring, Beck's phone buzzed and she scooped it up, half hoping, but half not, it would be Macy sending her a message. It was Liam. *What are you doing right now?*

She hesitated a moment before typing a response. *At JR's staring at the pool table. You up for a game?*

Anytime.

Head this way. I could use the company. She hit send before she could change her mind, reluctant though she was to admit she was lonely. It was hard going from a big, built-in family to just her. Thank God she had Liam and thank God he didn't have any hang-ups about meeting her in a queer bar. Jack used to always tease he'd join her there, but he didn't want to get everyone all excited. She hadn't had the heart to tell him he was unlikely to get everyone hot and bothered, but now she'd have no trouble telling him the truth. Lately, every time a memory of Jack surfaced it was laced with bitterness, making her wonder if any fondness she'd ever had for him was manufactured or if she was simply jaded by the shooting. The truth was likely somewhere in between, which was one of the reasons she was reluctant to talk to Macy or any other reporter. Would they catch the nuance, or would they only translate in stark relief whatever the relationship had been between them?

She didn't know and she needed to stop caring. Until Jack's trial, she needed to keep her head down and her mind focused on keeping her job and whatever else she had left. And then maybe, just maybe, she could find a way to rebuild.

Her glass was half empty when Liam scooped her up from behind in a giant bear hug. She pushed her way out of his arms. "Cut it out."

"What? I can't hug my little sister?" He made a show of looking around. "Or I can't hug my little sister in a bar where she might be scoping out a date?"

She punched him in the shoulder. "Take a better look. You're more likely to find a date in here than I am." She pointed at the barstool next to hers. "Sit. Order a beer. We're next in line for that table over there."

Dawson appeared at that moment, and he gave Liam a curious look before turning back to her with raised eyebrows. "I guess you like to switch up more than your drinks."

Normally, she'd find the observation of her personal life unwelcome, but his unobtrusive, but super observant manner was oddly comforting, and she was drawn in. "He's my brother. Liam, meet Dawson. Dawson, Liam."

Dawson stuck his hand out and Liam grasped it while Beck watched two of her worlds collide as Dawson gave Liam a long, slow, appraising once-over. It wasn't like Liam had never been out with her to a gay bar, but this place was more Cheers than Club Babylon and she didn't want any misconceptions about her brother to lead to bad feelings down the road that might make her feel uncomfortable about hanging out here. She grasped Liam's arm and waved in the direction of the pool table. "Looks like they're finishing up. Dawson, do you mind sending the beers over?"

She walked Liam over to the table and whispered, "Don't flirt with the guys here unless you mean it."

"You worried I'll out hustle you?" He shook his head. "Ain't going to happen."

"I'm worried you'll break some hearts and then I'll never be able to come back here without people asking where you are because they're pining away or pissed off."

Liam looked around. "This is a cool bar. When did you start hanging out here?"

"I've been here a few times." Exaggeration. She'd been here twice.

"Enough for you to be tight with the bartender?"

"He's a friendly guy. What can I say?" She was avoiding his real question, and he picked up his cue and chalked the tip—letting her know she was off the hook if she chose to be. She wanted to be off the hook, but she wanted to be honest with him more.

"I can't go to any of the old haunts. Too many cops, too much drama."

"I get it. You've always steered clear of gay bars. Just got me wondering is all." He took a deep drink from his beer. "You know there's a women's bar right around the corner."

"Since when did you become Mr. Gayborhood?"

"I'm hip." He grinned. "Actually, we had a group in from LA last week and Sue Ellen's was on their list of must-see venues for a potential app launch."

"I figured as much. I'm sure your group had a blast, but if I hang out there, it's only a matter of time before everyone figures out I'm a cop and then I'm the outcast. I get it—I really do, but it's easier here where I'm less likely to attract attention." She hesitated a moment while she considered whether to share the real reason she was at JR's today. "Besides, I was here to meet with Macy Moran."

"The reporter, Macy Moran?"

"That's the one."

Liam gave a low whistle. "Did you talk to her about the case?"

"No, not yet." She noted his eyebrow raise. "I'm considering it. She's going to write about it anyway. At least this way maybe I can control the narrative."

"Maybe. I mean I know she's top-notch, but have you read much of her stuff?"

She hadn't. Not because she didn't keep up with the news, but because most of what Macy tended to write were big feature pieces, the kind that the paper broke into several parts to keep readers hooked over the course of several weeks. To her mind, those didn't constitute news—they were more like Truman Capote style *In Cold Blood* kind of pieces, where she tried to get into the mind of all involved rather than straight to the truth of the matter. "Not a lot, but she has a good reputation."

"She does. It sounds like you've already made up your mind."

"I don't know, Liam. I'm damned either way. I'm spending my days doing data entry. Some promotion. Would it really hurt to put myself out there?"

"Hey, I've got your back no matter what you decide." He pointed at his chest. "Whatever you need."

She contemplated his offer and asked for a favor before either one of them could change their minds. "What are you doing Sunday?"

CHAPTER TEN

Macy hated this day. It wasn't the actual anniversary of Lauren's death, but it was close enough.

She parked in the lot behind Sue Ellen's and JR's, and walked through the crowd decked out in their rainbow gear, waving flags, and celebrating Pride, and wondered how many of them wouldn't make it home safely once the festivities were done. She thought about Janelle Silver and her father, and the other victims of the Parks and Rec Killer, but the one that occupied her mind the most wasn't here and never would be again. Today was the starkest reminder of Lauren's death, and she hated the shadow hanging over the festivities.

"Macy!"

She looked over her shoulder in time to see her old college roommate, Harrison Reynolds, before he scooped her up into a suffocating hug. She tolerated the embrace for a few seconds before she pushed away. "Okay, that's enough."

"Good to see you too, M."

She stared at his hands on his hips and the pout on his lips. His response might look exaggerated, but she knew she'd hurt his feelings. It occurred to her that he'd changed very little over the past ten years, something she probably would've noticed before if she took the time to get together more often. She spent a moment trying to remember if she'd seen him since this annual get-together last year, but no memory surfaced, and she realized texts and the occasional phone call had been their only contact. She was kind of a shitty friend. "I'm sorry, H. I'm a little prickly today."

"I suspect you're a little prickly every day, but lucky me, I don't have to see it." He held out his arm. "Shall we?"

She looked around. "Where's Donna?"

"She's already camped out in our usual spot. She sent me to look for you, and I was going to stop in JR's to grab a beer since I figured you'd be late, but here you are, being early. What's up?"

She wasn't about to admit she'd been hoping to run into Beck. Giving any small detail about Beck would send Harrison into an interrogation frenzy, so she pivoted. "Don't let me get in the way of you cruising the bar even if it is a little early in the day to pick someone to take home with you."

"As if. I may be going home with someone, but never the other way around."

"As if," she echoed, smiling, and matching his indignant tone.

"I love when you try to be like me," Harrison said as he grabbed her hand. "Come on. Let's grab our spot before Donna has to fight people for it."

She let him wind his fingers through hers and lead the way. This touch, unlike the bear hug, was oddly comforting, like he was in charge, so she didn't have to be. Maybe ceding a little control would be good for her. Maybe.

When they reached the sidewalk in front of JR's, she spotted Donna guarding three camp chairs and an ice chest like her life depended on it. She waved them over, and tentatively stepped toward Macy as if to hug her before she hesitated.

"It's okay," Macy said. "H here already hug-bombed me, so I'm desensitized."

Donna grinned and pulled her close. At first Macy tensed against the touch, but after a few seconds, she relaxed into the embrace, forgetting for a moment why they were hugging in the first place.

"I've missed you."

"Really?" Macy leaned back so she could see Donna's full expression when she answered.

"Really. Once a year isn't often enough."

Maybe it's too often. The thought shot in like a lightning bolt, but Macy filed it away. Donna and Harrison viewed this event as a way of healing, but they'd never shared her view there would be no healing until Lauren's killer was arrested, prosecuted, and punished for what he'd done. Meeting once a year at the place where it had all started wasn't going to bring Lauren back, and her time would be better spent doing concrete work to bring her justice.

Harrison held up a colorful can of beer from a local brewery. "Here, drink this. You look like your mind is going a million miles a minute."

"Her mind's always going that fast," Donna said. She waved a hand in front of Macy's face. "Relax a little. Lauren would want us to enjoy each other's company, don't you think?"

"You act like this is some kind of birthday party we gather to celebrate every year, and that Lauren's going to walk in at any moment and we'll all yell 'surprise' and crowd around her and exchange gifts and have a great time." She stopped, acutely conscious her voice was rising and people nearby were turning to look at them. "This isn't a celebration," she whispered harshly. "This isn't a party."

Harrison raised his eyebrows and jerked his head slightly. She turned to see Beck Ramsey standing behind her with a handsome guy holding a cooler, and she forced a smile.

"Looks like I arrived just in time for the fireworks," Beck said with a grin.

The sight of Beck smiling was startling enough, but the fact she was dressed in a sleeveless shirt and shorts that showed a serious length of well-toned leg was enough to cause Macy to forget what she'd been railing about. "You came?"

"Did you forget you invited me?"

She hadn't. Not really. She'd simply never considered Beck would actually show up. Macy cast a glance at the tall, handsome guy standing behind her. Beck was out, so she scratched husband and boyfriend from the list of possibilities. Wingman? She studied him closer until she recognized the resemblance—tall, blond, dark brown eyes. "Is this your brother?"

Beck stepped to the side and waved him closer. "Liam, meet Macy. Macy, this is my slightly older brother, Liam."

Harrison appeared at her side, practically salivating. He stuck his hand out toward Liam who shook it with a broad smile. "Nice to meet you. Come on, we've got chairs over here."

Macy watched him lead poor Liam away, certain her own chair was being sacrificed to Harrison's newest crush.

"Let me guess. Your 'hey, come to Pride on Sunday' was a throwaway remark." Beck ducked her head. "I get it. You probably don't make a habit of socializing with subjects you're writing about. I'll get Liam and we'll head out."

She took a step away, but Macy reached out and grabbed her arm. "No." She waited until Beck faced her. "I was serious when I invited you. And I'm not writing about you until you give the green light. Did you just give the green light?"

A hint of a smile appeared at the edge of Beck's lips. "Maybe. The day is young."

Macy play-wrote a note with her forefinger on her palm. "Not only is she a decorated cop, but she drives a hard bargain. Anything else I should know before we settle in?"

"I think that's it for now." Beck hefted the cooler in her hand. "Beer?"

She looked down at her hands and realized she'd never accepted the beer from Harrison. "Sure." While the growing crowd jostled them both, she watched Beck pop the tab on an icy can and hand it to her like they were the only two people standing on the sidewalk. Her fingers grazed Beck's as she took the can from her, and she took a deep swallow to distract from the intensity of the touch. It was hot outside, and she was hot inside, and it was going to be a long day trying to remain somewhat objective with Beck Ramsey standing next to her looking cool and refreshing and absolutely delicious.

"Who are your friends?"

"What?"

Beck pointed to where Donna and Harrison had surrounded Liam and the three of them were engaged in animated conversation. "Those people. The ones with the chairs and the conflict you all were discussing when Liam and I showed up."

"Oh, those people." Macy was stalling and she knew it. All she had to say was Harrison and Donna were college friends, but the big set of baggage that came with the question about how they'd managed to stay friends all these years wasn't easy, and it wasn't the kind of story you told to a virtual stranger standing in a crowd of rainbow-adorned other strangers on a hot summer day. She settled on a compromise. "Donna, Harrison, and I all shared a house while we were enrolled at Richards University. We get together every year for Pride."

"But not to celebrate?"

Macy's gut clenched. "Guess you heard us."

"You're not the only trained investigator here today." Beck raised her shoulders. "I didn't mean to listen in, but you were pretty exuberant."

"Tell you what. It's a long story, but all I want to do right now is drink this beer." She held up the can. "And get a tall person to catch beads for me when the parade starts. Are you in?"

"For the beer or the beads?"

"Both."

Beck nodded and hefted her cooler. "I have plenty of beer and a pretty decent reach. I'm in."

"See, I knew I liked you the moment we met." Macy motioned for Beck to follow and turned away before her objectivity melted in the heat. She needed the story with Beck in order to keep her editor happy, and if she had to share a few beers and watch a parade with her, how was that any different than the schmoozing that got press into top-tier arenas and other venues so they could gush about the home team or other local talent?

This was different and she knew it. But right now, she really didn't care.

❖

"Your new friend seems nice."

Beck took the beer Liam handed her and focused on it rather than the curious expression on his face. Yes, Macy did seem like a nice person, for a reporter, but there was an undercurrent of intensity in everything she said, and it served a warning that all might not be as it seemed. Macy's reference to the "long story" had been several hours ago, but she'd been unable to deduce anything more specific other than the fact that the bond holding Macy and her friends together ran deeper and darker than a shared college experience. She cast a glance over at the three of them, huddled together in whispered conversation. "I guess so."

"Nice enough to get you to leave the house for something other than work and your morning run."

"I guess I'm tired of hiding out, and this seemed like as good a place as any to take the first step."

"I'd say so. I doubt anyone would even recognize you here, looking all casual."

He was right. Out of uniform, with her hair down, sporting Wayfarers instead of Aviators, and a beer in her hand, she fit right in with the teeming crowd of party people. No one would suspect she was a cop. Minutes earlier, one of the patrol cops from the White Rock substation had passed right by her without a second glance, and the anonymity, after weeks in the spotlight, was a welcome relief. "It is kind of nice, flying under the radar." She gestured toward Macy and her friends. "What do you make of them?"

"Are you asking me because you're interested as a cop or for some other reason?"

"What difference does it make?"

"Well, there's a big difference between dating and forensics."

"It's not a date. I told you, she's been trying to interview me since the preliminary hearing in Jack's case."

"Interesting."

"I hate when you do that."

"Do what?"

"Act like you know more about a situation than I do when I'm the one who's in it."

"For a trained observer, you have a huge blind spot. She may be a reporter, but she's interested in more than a story here."

Was she? She cycled back through her interactions with Macy, but the only signal she'd gotten that Macy wanted more was the straightforward request she'd made to get a look at some cold case files. "It's not what you think. She does want more, but it's work-related, not personal."

"If you say so." He tore his gaze from Macy and her friends and faced her. "She seems like she's got a bit of a whirlwind thing going on. Like it's hard to focus. Other than that, I stand by my initial assessment. Nice person, attractive. I approve."

She punched him in the arm. "I didn't ask for your approval. And," she pointed in the direction of Macy and her friends, "this isn't what you keep trying to make it out to be."

"You may not have asked for my approval, but I'm happy to give it. It's what big brothers do."

A voice from behind Beck called out. "Are you two over us?"

She turned to see Harrison standing behind her, but his eyes were on Liam because of course they were. "Not completely," she said, keeping her expression neutral. "Seriously, we're thinking of making the rounds." She stuck out her hand. "It was nice to meet you. Say bye to Macy for us." There, that should show Liam she wasn't pining after anyone. She grabbed Liam's arm and steered him away, ignoring Harrison's crestfallen face.

"I can't believe you're ditching them when you just got here," Liam whispered as they walked away. "You could use a new set of friends about now."

She hid her regret about leaving Macy and her friends because what was the point? "Macy's not a friend. She's a reporter who wants a story. And she didn't exactly invite me to join them. She gave me a little grief about never having attended Pride for fun and I decided to come down and see how it felt to be a civilian during the big party." She glanced around at the growing crowd of hot, sweaty bodies. Everyone was drinking and laughing and excited about the parade. Was she the only one here suffocating from the tight quarters, on guard against the vulnerabilities of the inhibited crowd? "I shouldn't have come."

"I don't know about that. You may need another beer before you can properly assess." He pointed at the bar behind them. "Woody's. Perfect. Let's go in there and cool off. Maybe you'll meet the love of your life inside."

"Way more likely to happen to you, but cooling off sounds good." She started to follow him up the stairs when she heard someone call her name. She turned to see Macy standing at the bottom of the steps. "Hi," she said, feeling silly for having ducked out on her. "We're discussing going inside to cool off."

"May I talk to you a minute?" Macy asked. "It'll only take a second."

Beck looked back up at Liam who nodded. "It's cool. I'll see you inside." He grinned. "Or not."

She shook her head and turned to Macy, waiting to hear what she had to say.

"I'm not going to try and interview you here," Macy said. "In case that's why you ditched us."

Beck hunched her shoulders. "I get it. It's your job. I'm not ready to commit, and now that I'm here, I figured I should try and enjoy myself." She looked out over the crowd, and her growing unease prompted her to share. "It's not easy."

"I imagine. You're used to working Pride, not enjoying it. Bet you see a possible active shooter in every person carrying a backpack."

"Something like that." It was nice to have someone get her, but she had to be careful not to mistake observation for friendship. "Liam and I are headed in here for a bit. Might help."

"Believe it or not today is really stressful for me too. I mean I'm not on hyper vigilant lookout for a potential shooter or bomb threat like you, but it's hard for me to be here pretending to celebrate."

The admission sounded like a volley of friendship, an attempt to share an experience, but Beck went on alert lest she fall into a trap. "Is that so?"

"It is. If you stick around, I'll tell you about it. One personal story for another. It's only fair, right?"

She should leave. No story was worth an entanglement that pricked the hairs on her neck, and whatever Macy had to say sounded ominous. Why did she even care? If Macy was uncomfortable being here, she should leave. Plain and simple.

But whatever was on Macy's mind wasn't plain or simple. She could tell by the lurking pain in Macy's eyes and the way she tucked into herself when she alluded to whatever was bothering her. Okay, so she cared enough to notice those things, but that didn't mean she had to stick around.

Before she could give her answer, the cloud disappeared, and Macy's face brightened into a smile. "But that's for later," she said. "Right now, there's beer to drink and beads to catch, and Donna packed excellent snacks."

When Macy slid her arm around her waist, Beck was surprised when she didn't recoil at the uninvited embrace, and when Macy led her back to the spot her friends had staked out, she was compelled to follow. She didn't know why, and she didn't know how, but she was drawn to this woman and she wanted to hear her story even if she had to endure an entire day of hot, sweaty festival goers to get to it.

CHAPTER ELEVEN

We were seniors at Richards University," Macy said, her voice low but still distinct in the crowded, noisy bar. "Richards was a great place to go to school. It's easy, when you're on campus to forget you're right here in the middle of the city, but when you're ready to live a little, all of Dallas is mere minutes away."

Beck nodded and while she waited for Macy to continue, she took a drink from her beer and made a mental note to rideshare home. It had been a long, hot day and she'd consumed more than she was used to, but it wasn't until she took a seat at the bar that she started to feel the effects. Liam had offered her a ride when he'd left a couple of hours before, but curiosity about Macy's story convinced her to decline. Harrison and Donna were roaming Cedar Springs, on a scouting mission to find out which bar was playing the best dance music and report back. Meanwhile, she and Macy had adjourned to JR's where Dawson kicked a couple of hipsters off of their barstools to make room for them. Score one for her new friendship with Dawson.

"I went to UT," she said when Macy seemed stalled. "The school was great, but Austin was the big draw. I can relate to wanting to be in the thick of things."

Macy nodded but still didn't say anything. Beck noticed she'd been doing a lot of that since they'd walked into the bar, like she was conserving her words for the story she was about to tell. A story Beck was now dying to hear. She hoped the tale lived up to the hype, but mostly she was just curious what Macy thought made good information currency. Was she about to give a confession of sorts?

Quit playing detective. The inner voice was strong, and it wriggled under her skin. She was a detective—a role she'd aspired to, but now that she'd made it, there was nothing to detect, and she wasn't about to begrudge herself the opportunity to test her skill against whatever Macy was about to tell her. First rule, give the witness space to talk. Too often investigators filled the silent pauses with words of their own, designed to fill in the blanks, and too often they led the story in a completely different direction than the witness intended or worse yet, never drilled deep on the details, assuming the narrative they'd shaped was fully formed. Macy would talk when she was ready, and no amount of pushing would change her truth.

"Lauren was the best kind of friend. We met freshman year, matched to a room at Jordan Hall, and instantly clicked. We were lucky. Other roommates argued and fought, but we managed to live together in the fifteen-by-fifteen space like we were an old couple who'd learned to navigate each other's habits over a lifetime." Macy stopped and stared right into Beck's eyes. "Go on, ask."

The question was a dare, but Beck had never shied away from getting to the truth. Besides, she was genuinely curious. "Were you lovers?"

"No. Insert heavy sigh here. Don't get me wrong, after a few weeks of living together I had a serious crush." Macy reached into her pocket, pulled out a small credit card wallet, and reached behind her driver's license. She fished out a picture and handed it to Beck. "I think you can see why."

Lauren was a stunner. Waves of dark brown hair cascaded around her shoulders, and her eyes were smoky gray-green with a hint of a flirty smile—dangerous combo. "She's beautiful."

"Inside and out." Macy held out her hand for the picture, her fingers twitching slightly as Beck delayed, taking one more glance. When she finally handed it back, Macy hastily shoved it back in her wallet and shoved the wallet back in her pocket. "But a crush is all it ever was. We became fast friends and never crossed that line."

Was she hearing a wistful tone in Macy's voice? Whatever it was, Macy wasn't interested in discussing it right now and Beck decided not to press. "When did you meet Harrison and Donna?"

"Lauren and I met them at a Sig Ep mixer." Macy frowned. "I know, I know. Lauren had done some philanthropy work with them while she was working with the North Texas Food Bank, and they were presenting the food bank with one of those big, blown-up checks. I went along for moral support. Donna went along, hoping to meet cute frat guys, and Harrison was there as her wingman. We bonded over the bottle of Tito's I snuck in, so we didn't have to stand in line at the keg. The four of us started hanging out later and we all got along, so junior year, we decided to ditch the dorms and get a house together."

Beck knew the story was headed somewhere dark. Lauren's absence from today's festivities told her that much, but she wanted to know the details if only to have some insight into Macy's world view. She sensed Macy needed to tell this story in bite-sized pieces to get through it, so she helped her along. "I bet four of you renting a house was cheaper than the dorms."

"And the food's better. Only drawback is you have to cook it yourself. Donna's the *Top Chef* wannabe in the group so we all chipped in on groceries and let her feed us. If it were up to me, we would've all starved."

"Remind me not to accept any dinner invitations from you."

Macy smiled at the words and Beck instantly regretted the familiarity, but it was silly really. Here she was sitting in a bar, drinking beer with a reporter after spending the entire day cheering at floats and jumping for beads. Lines had already been crossed. What were a few more? She cleared her throat and refocused the conversation on Macy's story. "What happened to Lauren?"

Macy's smile disappeared and she bit her bottom lip and looked off to the right, over Beck's shoulder, like her next lines were on the wall behind her. Beck wanted to say something to nudge her along but knew the best way to get a full story was to wait, letting the silence between them rise to overflowing. This wasn't an interrogation, but the skills were the same. Thankfully, she didn't have to wait long.

❖

"It was a Sunday. Like this one. We'd spent all day at Pride. Lauren, Donna, Harrison, and I." Macy took a drink from her beer while she contemplated her next words. She knew exactly what to say—the details were burned in her brain after she'd reviewed them every single day since it had happened, but she'd never told the story to someone who didn't already know parts of it, and she wanted to make sure she didn't miss a single detail in the telling.

"Lauren hadn't wanted to go with us to Pride. She had a date that night. It was her first date with this guy, Joel, and she didn't want to get all hot and sweaty and have to go home and shower before going out."

"She was straight?" Beck asked, sounding surprised.

"Lauren didn't like labels. She dated whoever she was attracted to in the moment. None of us knew this guy. She met him in her astronomy class. She liked to joke that their meeting was written in the stars. He apparently didn't get the memo because he waited until the semester ended before asking her out."

"So, she decided to go to Pride with you after all."

Macy recognized the move-on tactic since she'd used it plenty of times in the past when interviewing subjects who tended to ramble. She had never considered herself a rambler, but writing about this subject was one thing and speaking the words out loud was something altogether different. "Yes. She was frequently plagued by FOMO. She rode down here with me, and the plan was she'd get a cab home when she was ready to go."

"Did she?"

Macy wanted to hate the direct, pinpointed questions, but she appreciated Beck's style too much to resent the fact it was being used on her. "I don't know. She walked away from us at the corner of Knight and Cedar Springs. I never saw her alive again."

And that was it. The end of one story and the beginning of another. Anticipating Beck's next question, she plunged ahead. "A jogger found her body Monday morning in the wooded area near the Big Thicket," she said, referring to one of the park buildings on White Rock Lake. "She was bound and strangled just like the others—the fifth victim of the Parks and Rec Killer."

"The last one, right?"

Macy stared Beck in the eyes, but nothing she saw indicated she was making a foregone conclusion. "The last one, at the time." She braced for a challenge, but Beck only sighed and shook her head.

"I'm so sorry for your loss," she said. "That must have been devastating."

Beck's words were delivered with a pained expression that struck Macy as genuine, and not at all what she'd been expecting. "It was. Is."

"Is that why you decided to become an investigative journalist?"

"Partly. I've always had an interest in Nancy Drew-like endeavors, but Lauren's death was definitely a motivating factor."

"And you're writing about it now?"

"It's the tenth anniversary." Beck nodded in response and Macy almost decided to let the statement lie and not mention anything else, but she couldn't resist gauging her reaction even if it meant Beck decided she was crazy. "And I think he's back."

Beck swallowed her beer and calmly set the bottle on the bar before facing her with a neutral expression. Unflappable. No wonder she'd been a commended cop and had been promoted to detective. It was clear she was calm, cool, and controlled, which made Macy even more interested in getting her take on her brewing theory. "The woman you found near White Rock Lake? I'd bet money she's another victim. Slight differences in the crime scene, but she was in her early twenties, just like the others."

"Who's assigned to the case?"

"Claire Hanlon."

"But she's a squad commander."

"I know, and I think it's telling that she would take a personal interest in this case. Do you know her?"

"Not well. Just to speak to in passing. What does she think of your theory?"

"I'm waiting until she has the final report back from the ME to bring it up. It'll be harder for her to dismiss me outright then."

"But you're convinced the recent case is connected to the deaths from ten years ago."

She barely detected the hint of incredulity, but it was there. She'd expected it, but it was disappointing nevertheless. "I do. And I'm going to prove it."

"And I'm your gateway to the cold case files."

"Yes. I mean I filed a FOIA request, so it's not like I'm trying to skirt around authority here. I'm entitled to see those old reports."

Beck took a deep drink from her beer. "I have to say, with all the buildup, I was kind of expecting a longer story."

Macy met her stare, determined not to flinch. The story was ten years long, but she didn't know Beck well enough to tell her the whole thing, or maybe she simply didn't want to chase her away with the details. Whatever the case, she'd shared enough today. If Beck wouldn't help her, she'd find another way. She always did. "Hey, if you don't want to help solve this case, that's fine. I'm sure there's some other cop who cares more about the truth than placating their boss."

"Do people usually respond well when you bait them like this?"

Beck delivered the words with a smile, but it was a fair question. "Who says I use this tactic with anyone else?"

"Well, if you don't, I guess that makes me special."

The smile again, but this time it was layered with flirtation or at least what Macy figured was flirtation. It had been a long time since she'd spent time in the company of a woman she was attracted to, let alone twice in one week. Hell, she rarely spent time in the company of anyone other than the citizen detectives in the online chat that had become her lifeline over the years. It was different being around people in real life, and while the evenings she'd spent with Beck could hardly be categorized as dates, there was no denying the magnetic pull she experienced in Beck's presence. Did Beck feel it too? It was hard to imagine she enjoyed being hounded by a reporter. Could it be she was interested in something more? "You seem pretty special." Not the smoothest rejoinder, but better than sitting and staring.

"Oh yeah, and why's that?"

"You showed up today when I know it had to be uncomfortable. I caught you looking around every time someone walked by with a cooler. You were on guard even while you were acting like you were totally engaged in conversation with my friends. And speaking of friends, I know Donna and Harrison can be a bit much."

Beck laughed. "And you're not?"

"What? Seriously?"

"You can be a little intense. Surely you know this."

She did, but the only people who ever said it to her face were her best friends, never the women she dated, though she figured that was one of the reasons they stopped calling, texting, picking up the phone. "Occupational hazard. Tell me you haven't had the same complaint from the people in your life."

Beck raised her hands in surrender. "True. True. But I'm working on it."

"Let me know what you figure out. I do my best work when I'm hyper focused."

"And you're always hyper focused."

Beck didn't know her well enough to draw that conclusion, but it didn't make it any less true. Harrison joked she needed a TA group, Truth Anonymous, where people admitted their powerlessness over the inability to solve mysteries. She wasn't ready to admit the mystery couldn't be solved. Not by a long shot, but she was interested in a new mystery and that was the woman seated right next to her. Maybe she should ditch the story about Beck and ask her out instead. Jerry would lose his mind, but she'd be able to calm him down eventually. And the corporate schmucks could kiss her ass.

"I'll do it."

Beck's words didn't compute. Had Beck read her mind just now? "What?"

"I'll give you the interview. And I'll look up the case files, but I can't promise I can do more than give you whatever you'd be entitled to anyway from your FOIA request."

"That's great," she said, summoning enthusiasm she didn't feel. Beck was giving her everything she'd asked for, and under other circumstances, she'd count it as a win. So why was she left feeling unsatisfied?

CHAPTER TWELVE

Monday morning, Beck woke to the sound of pans rattling in the kitchen. She pulled on a pair of boxers and a T-shirt and wandered out to Liam's kitchen to find him adjusting the flame on the gas stovetop. "What is happening?"

"I'm making breakfast." He pointed to a French press on the counter. "Coffee's ready. Help yourself."

Relieved at the sight of the full press, she wandered over, poured a cup, and took a deep swallow. "I was thinking it's time I start staying at my own place, but then I'd miss you waiting on me." She held up the cup. "This is delicious."

"You know you're welcome here anytime." He pointed at the coffee. "It's some new brew a client is trying out. I'm drinking my way through the few pounds they gave me while I figure out ad copy." He poured some batter onto a griddle and not very artfully changed the subject. "Your new friends are nice."

Beck went on alert at the seemingly innocuous statement. She'd slept in later than normal, even skipping her usual run, and now she was wishing she was more alert for the question and answer portion of the morning after.

"They aren't my friends. And why are you making pancakes on a Monday morning?"

"They seemed like they were. And I'm making pancakes because we both had a lot of beer yesterday and I figured we could use something to soak it up."

She set her coffee mug down and stretched her arms above her head. "You've got that right. About the pancakes I mean. As for Harrison and Donna, they're Macy's friends."

"And what's Macy to you?"

Beck wished he'd finish the damn pancakes so they could stuff their face with something other than this uncomfortable conversation. "Do you have maple syrup? The good kind, not that maple flavored crap."

He pointed at the cabinet behind her with his spatula. "Second shelf. Brand new bottle."

She turned to the cabinet and took her time retrieving the syrup because she sensed breakfast was mostly about pumping her for information about what had happened at Pride after he bailed.

When she'd finally used up an irrational amount of time fetching the syrup, she set it on the table and squared off with Liam. "You know if you want to know what's going on you could've stuck around."

"I was giving you and Macy some alone time," he replied without missing a beat. "See what a nice guy I am?"

"You're a pain in the ass is what you are. She's trying to interview me for the paper. She wants an exclusive. That's it." She spun her forefinger in a circle. "All that other crap in your head is make-believe."

He shoveled pancakes into a perilously high stack on the platter. "I have empirical evidence to suggest otherwise."

"Here we go."

"Seriously, Beck." He pointed to the desk in the corner. "Hand me my phone."

She strode over the to the desk and retrieved his phone. A moment later, he held it up to show her a series of photos. The first few were of Harrison, Donna, and Macy, enjoying Pride, but smack in the middle were several pictures of her and Macy. Standing close. Sharing a beer. Exchanging whispered conversations. She closed her eyes for a moment and remembered the day. She'd had fun for the first time in a while, and for a few hours, she forgot all about the fact the rest of her life had turned upside down. Despite the crowds and the heat, it had been the best day she'd had in a long time, and looking at the pictures, it did appear she and Macy were getting along fabulously. She grabbed the phone from Liam's hand. "Don't believe everything you see."

"Is that the route you're going to take? Because I'm thinking it's antithetical to your well-honed detecting skills. Aren't you always looking for an eyewitness?"

"They aren't always reliable." As she spoke the words, she got the irony. She was in the position she was in because she was certain she'd seen Jack shoot an unarmed victim. But she was a trained observer, not a pedestrian on the street who may have caught a glimpse of something but didn't note full detail because they hadn't been expecting to see something go down and weren't prepared or trained to register all of the details. "In fact, eyewitnesses are notoriously unreliable, but they sure are convincing to juries." She pointed at the phone. "Macy's nice enough, but it's business. I promise."

"She's cute too."

Cute wasn't how she'd describe Macy, but correcting Liam would only give him more reason to tease her. Macy was attractive, but not in a cute and sweet way. Her magnetism came from the fact she was fierce and fiery. If Macy wasn't a reporter intent on getting her to spill her guts, she might be inclined to ask her out. But the situation was what it was, and business was all it could ever be between them. The casual flirtation at yesterday's Pride celebration was a fluke and it wasn't going to be repeated. "Speaking of attraction, Harrison thought you were pretty cute."

"If I was into guys, I'd totally go for him, but alas I felt nothing more than friendship. He's pretty cool."

"I love how you don't get freaked out when a guy finds you attractive."

"Why would I? It's a compliment, right?"

"It is, but you'd be surprised how many gay bashings start exactly that way."

"That's shitty. Besides, it could just as easily happen to me."

"You are the quintessential metrosexual, for sure."

"I'm definitely taking that as a compliment."

"Good, because it is. Anyway, I'm glad you're not an asshole since that would mean I wouldn't spend any time with you, and I'd sure miss these pancakes."

He shoved a plate her way. "Eat up."

She groaned at the first bite. She hadn't been eating much lately—since the shooting. Every time she did, she thought about how Aldridge would never take another breath, eat another meal. About how Jack's future was ruined and how hers might be, and her appetite gave way to a wave of nauseous guilt. But not today. Today, she ate a big stack of pancakes and enjoyed every bite, wondering if agreeing to the interview with Macy was the source of her relief. "I decided to give an interview to the paper."

Liam paused mid-bite and stared her down. "Really? Macy's paper, I presume?"

"That's the one." She took another bite to avoid his penetrating gaze.

"Okay." He resumed eating but didn't look away.

"I can tell you have an opinion. Go ahead and dish."

"It's really not my business."

"Since when has that ever stopped you?"

He rolled his eyes. "Fine. It might be awkward dating her if she's going to write an exposé on your case."

She set her fork down, her appetite quickly fading. "First off, there is no dating. This is a business arrangement. Second, she's writing a profile piece, not an exposé."

"Yeah, okay."

"What's the deal, Liam? First, you tell me how great she is and now you're warning me away from her?"

"Name a journalist that's not going to seize on a bigger story if there's one to be had."

"I can handle myself."

"Under most circumstances, my money would be all on you."

"There's a big but at the end of that sentence."

"This isn't most circumstances. Have you talked to your union rep about this?"

"Since when do you know anything about union reps?"

He pushed his plate aside. "You forget, I'm a master in the art of googling. Since you're not big on sharing details, I did a little research of my own. I guess I'm concerned about any of Jack's case blowing back on you."

"It won't."

"Are you sure?"

She stared into his big brown, caring eyes and was a little bit touched by his concern, but it still agitated her, and she wasn't sure why. Yes, she wasn't big on sharing the nitty-gritty of her job with him, but that had stemmed from a lifetime of shoving her own feelings aside in the name of responsibility. Of all people, he should get that, but for some reason, the death of their mother had affected them in completely opposite ways. She'd become taciturn and he overshared with anyone who'd listen. She wouldn't change a thing about Liam, but she couldn't change her own method of coping simply because he'd chosen a different way to deal.

She stared at him and injected as much sincerity as she could muster into her response. "I'm sure."

He smiled and nodded, but she could tell he didn't entirely believe her, which was fine because when she thought about Macy's intense gaze focused completely on her, she wasn't certain she believed herself.

Macy stood in front of her fridge as if by continuing to stare at the empty shelves, food would suddenly materialize. Finally, she shut the door and focused her energy on making a coffee in the Nespresso machine Harrison had given her for her birthday last year. She kept a sizable volume of the pods on hand because unlike all the other groceries she bought, they didn't go bad before she got around to doing anything with them. Good thing she liked her coffee black.

While she waited for the cup to brew, she sent a text to Jerry to let him know she'd be working from home today. She didn't tell him Beck had agreed to the interview because then he'd give her a hard and fast deadline and be all over her until she turned the story in, but she did tell him she was close to getting what he wanted. Satisfied he was placated enough not to bother her for the rest of the day, she placed a basic grocery order on her phone. She didn't cook, but it helped to have a few staples on hand for days she chose to work from home. Usually, she skipped breakfast, but she hadn't had a lot to eat yesterday, and between the heat and the beer, she'd woken up this morning dehydrated and hungry.

When the coffee finished brewing, she wandered to the extra bedroom she'd converted into a home office. Holding her mug in one hand, she inserted a key in the lock and opened the door. As always, she took a moment to look around and make sure everything was exactly the way she'd left it. Silly really, since she kept the room locked, but being cautious had become a habit and she'd worked way too hard to assemble the information contained in this room to risk anything happening to it.

Her desk was covered with scraps of paper—news articles, notes, random other bits of information. Puzzle pieces waiting to be assembled. If only she had a box with the picture on it to go by, but all she had was confidence that the answer was within her grasp which fueled her desire to keep looking.

She set her mug on the table, signed on to her computer, and logged on to the website for Unfrozen. She didn't care for the name since it sounded like the lesser twin of a Disney movie, but it was the best crowd-sourced network of volunteer sleuths around, and she'd joined up several years ago when it was first formed.

She spent a few minutes reviewing the chat log from the weekend, but there were no new posts related to the Parks and Rec Killer, and no recent hits on her collection of search terms. She pulled up the notes app on her phone and typed in everything she'd learned so far about the body the jogger had discovered at White Rock Lake.

Jody Nelson had celebrated her twenty-second birthday the day before her last bike ride at the lake. According to security camera footage, she'd entered the trail near Richards University around seven on the evening before her body was found. Once she was off campus, the trail of hard evidence ended. According to Detective Hanlon, no one had come forward with any information about having seen Jody while she was riding the trail on the lake. Macy knew Claire would've tried hard to find witnesses, but she still found it hard to believe no one had seen Jody on the trail that night, especially since the area where her body had been found was several miles away from where she'd entered the trail. On a summer night in the kind of good weather they'd had that week, there would've been dozens of other cyclists, joggers, and walkers on the trail. The police found Jody's bike in one of the tributaries that fed into the lake about fifty feet from her body, but otherwise it was like she'd vanished off the trail without even a puff of smoke to mark the occasion.

Macy shook her head. Someone had to have seen something relevant to solving the case. She opened up a new chat and typed the subject line: *Is the Parks and Rec Killer Back in Action?*

Jody Nelson, twenty-two-year-old student at Richards University, was found dead at White Rock Lake over a week ago. Police don't have any leads, but she was hog-tied and strangled. Sound familiar?

She resisted the urge to type more, to fill in the space on the screen with her own theories. She knew in her gut he was back in action, but better to let the people on this page come to that realization themselves since it would make them more invested in the hunt.

While she waited for a reaction, she stood and walked over to the wall she'd made into a bulletin board. Photos of the Parks and Rec Killer's known victims lined the top of the board like great-grandparents on a family tree with lines drawn below to connect the specific facts of their case and display any facts they might have in common with the others. This wall represented years of effort, a stark boundary between the past and present, and it had come to define her entire view of the world. This wall was the story, and as soon as she filled in the missing pieces, she could write "the end."

Which brought her back to Beck. Beck had agreed to the story and whether her consent had been fueled by too much sun or too much beer, she was going to hold Beck to the bargain. Somewhere in those cold case files there was a clue, a sign, a pattern. Something the detectives had missed. But if she had access, she knew she could find answers. She'd been looking at the facts much longer than all the detectives originally assigned to the case had, combined. And she was the only one determined to stay on the case until it was solved.

Her computer dinged to alert her to a message. She strode over to it, tempering her excitement, knowing it was likely nothing more than the barrage of comments that come when someone tossed out a new theory on a case. Lots of noise, little substance. She slid into her chair and enlarged the chat box. The comments were coming in fast and hard:

Guy's probably dead by now.

More likely a copycat.

I heard there were signs of a struggle. PNRK? Never.

The consensus was she was way off base. And that was the point of these chats, right? Everyone could float their theory and get real time feedback from a bunch of people engaged in the same pursuit—finding the truth. She kept scrolling encountering a combination of questions about her reasoning to comments about her IQ. She was about to sign off when another ding sounded, and a new comment appeared.

I think you're on to something.

She checked the profile name: Huntsman363. She seen his posts before, and they'd exchanged messages too. Of course, she didn't know Huntsman363's gender, but her gut told her he was male. Her fingers hovered over the keys while she mentally composed a reply designed to keep him talking, but he beat her to it.

It's the ten-year anniversary. Maybe he's sentimental.

She hadn't voiced those words, but she'd thought them several times since the morning she'd stood out at White Rock Lake, staring at Jody Nelson's lifeless body.

It's not quite the anniversary. We need to stay on guard.

The response came within seconds of her typing the last word.

He needs to be stopped.

He did need to be stopped. Macy flashed to an image of Beck sitting next to her at JR's. The fun and the beer they'd shared that day had started out as way to suck up to Beck, to get her to agree to the interview for information exchange, but by the end of the evening, her goal had shifted, and as much as anything else, she wanted to hang out with Beck to get to know her. Not just cop her, but all of her. And that was a problem because if her goal was putting away the Parks and Rec Killer, her only focus should be on the ways in which Beck could help her solve these cases, not how Beck made her feel.

Renewing her commitment to finding the killer injected her with a boost of confidence. She read Huntsman363's last comment and stretched her fingers over the keys.

On it.

CHAPTER THIRTEEN

Thursday afternoon, Beck walked by Mendoza's office and subtly glanced inside as she strode past. She hadn't seen a sign of her all day, but she wanted to make extra sure Mendoza wouldn't pop up while she was out.

Foster was sitting at his desk and looked up when she walked in. "You done with all the new files?"

"Yep. Every last one."

He gave a low whistle. "I'm impressed."

She'd run through the new files quickly now that she was in a rhythm, but she still had plenty of the backlogged work waiting, having established a method of working through one box of old, then one box of new, rotating back and forth to keep a balance between being bored out of her mind by antiquated files and intrigued by cases that had a chance of catching fresh eyes.

Not that it really mattered if there was a method at all since no one was doing anything with the information other than cataloguing it. A not very well-trained monkey could do what she was doing, and the idea she was stuck here indefinitely for doing the right thing on the street galled her. But Foster wasn't to blame and taking it out on him wasn't going to solve her problems. "Thanks. I guess you could say I'm in a groove." She glanced back at Mendoza's office door. "Is she coming in today?"

"Why? You thinking about playing hooky?"

The insight was jarring, but she smiled to cover. "As if. I've got an appointment." She cast about for an excuse. "You know, to talk about *the* case," she added, content to let him think she was visiting the prosecutor on Jack's case rather than a reporter.

He waved his hands in a shooing motion. "Go, go. Nothing's happening here that can't wait."

She took his advice and rushed out of the office. Thankfully, for her anyway, Foster's doctor had delayed his return to active duty, meaning he was available to serve as her buffer for a while longer. If she had to deal with Mendoza one on one for the duration of her time here, she might wind up quitting the force.

Her meeting with Macy was on the other side of town, but she made it to the Lakewood branch of the library in record time. She was glancing around, looking for Macy in the lobby, when she felt a tap on her shoulder. She turned to face a slender, attractive redhead with an easy smile.

"Detective Ramsey?"

This stranger was the first person to use her new title as an address, and it was disconcerting. Was she really a detective when she wasn't doing any detecting? She nodded slowly while she chewed on the existential question.

"Follow me, please."

The woman started walking into the belly of the library, leading her past rows of books and carrels and a group of children who were seated in a circle, listening to a story. Soon, they were standing in front of a closed door in the very back of the building. The woman knocked on the door, two quick raps, and after a few seconds, opened the door a few inches. At her urging, Beck stepped forward and peered inside to find Macy seated at a table that filled the small space.

"Sorry for the subterfuge," Macy said with a smile, "but I figured you'd appreciate us being circumspect." She waved at the redhead. "Thanks, Susan."

Susan waved as she walked away, and Beck walked into the room and shut the door behind her. "Impressive. Do you have people ready and willing to do your bidding everywhere you go?"

Macy cocked her head. "Interesting question. Let's just say that I find it's a good idea to make friends with as many people as I can in all walks of life because you never know when you're going to need a particular kind of thing. Susan is my favorite librarian. She's great at helping me with research and I'd put her up against any *Jeopardy* contestant—past, current, future."

"High praise indeed."

Macy pointed to the chair across from her and Beck sat down. "I imagine it's the same for cops. I'm sure you cultivated plenty of sources during your time in patrol."

"Lot of good that will do me now." Beck saw Macy perk up at the admission, and she wished she'd been more careful with her response. Maybe Liam was right, and giving this interview was a mistake.

"I'm sure it sucks to get a promotion and not be able to do the job you've worked to achieve."

Beck searched Macy's face for any sign she was baiting her, but all she read there was genuine compassion—something she hadn't received from anyone other than Liam since the shooting. No one except the counselor she'd been forced to see as a condition of keeping her job, had bothered to check in with her about how Jack's actions had affected her. She'd been standing right there when the gun went off. Watched as the bullet ripped through Aldridge's body. She'd frantically called for an ambulance while scrambling to save his life. She may not be facing jail time for what happened, but the events of that night had upended her career, made her a pariah, and left her with a permanent emotional scar. "It sucks" was an entirely accurate way of summarizing her current situation. She wished she'd never agreed to this interview while at the same time she was eager to tell her own story. Best to plunge in. She crossed her legs. "This is an interesting place to choose for a meeting."

"I love libraries, don't you?" Macy didn't wait for an answer. "Not only are they treasure troves of information, but most of the people who come here are wrapped up in their own needs—research, using the computers to access the internet, finding their next great read. And they have these soundproof rooms, perfect for having private conversations."

"Except this conversation isn't private." Beck leaned back in her chair and met Macy's intense gaze. "Right? You're here to get the scoop on what happened the night of the shooting and publish it for all the world to see."

"I think you overestimate the size of our readership."

Beck chafed at her teasing tone. "You know what I mean. Your interest in me only extends to an exclusive that will drive people to buy the paper, click on a link, whatever."

"You want me to say I care about you as a person?"

Did she? And if she did, why? She swallowed a lump in her throat and shook her head. She was being ridiculous. Emotional. She was here to give her perspective to a story that had gotten completely out of control, but she knew in her heart, she wouldn't be telling her side to just any reporter. So why now and why Macy?

Because your gut tells you you can trust her. She couldn't articulate why, but she knew it was true. Over the course of the past few days, she'd read everything she could find that Macy had written, and her overall impression was that Macy dug deep to find the truth, or as close an approximation as was possible. Beck wasn't naive enough to think the truth was black-and-white, but sussing out all the shades of gray was a rare trait and Macy had it in spades. She took a deep breath and plunged in. "What do you want to know?"

Macy studied her for a moment, like she was trying to figure out what to ask, but the first question out of her mouth was ostensibly innocuous. "Why did you decide to become a cop?"

Beck let out a breath. "My mom was a cop. Houston PD. She was killed in the line of duty, but I'm thinking you already know that if you're half the reporter people say you are."

Macy met her stare and nodded slowly. "I read about it, and I'm sorry for your loss. You were young when it happened, right?"

"I was thirteen. Liam was sixteen. She was responding to a domestic disturbance call. Those are always a crap shoot. Of course, I didn't know that at the time." She swallowed hard against the lump in her throat that formed every time she had to talk about her mother. "I'm sure you read that our dad lost it when she died. He never recovered." A nice way to gloss over years of drunken, sobbing fits that characterized her teenage years. She could never bring anyone home for fear he would lose it in front of company. It was hard to make friends when your only parent acted like an unpredictable, emotionally damaged child. One day he'd be overly solicitous and another he'd throw dishes across the room, claiming the world was out to get him.

"In light of what happened to your mother, some people might have chosen a job that had nothing to do with law enforcement," Macy said.

"Like what? Bank robber? Why wouldn't I want to pursue an occupation that trained me to get bad guys?"

"Did it?"

"Did it what?"

"Train you to get bad guys?"

"Just because Jack did what he did, doesn't mean the rest of us aren't focused on helping people."

"So, you became a cop to help people?"

Why hadn't she anticipated and better prepared for this question? Beck mentally kicked herself, while she cycled through potential answers. Yes, she wanted to help people. Yes, she'd always viewed cops as the good guys, the ones you ran to when you were in trouble, knowing they would always have your back, be your protector. The words sounded cheesy when she replayed them in her head, but cheesy or not, the sentiment was true. Her mother had worked a beat just like she had, for many years, and she'd taken for granted she was the protector, never in need of protection herself. The day her mother's commanding officer had come to the house to break the news, her own expectations had been shattered, but it had also shifted her perspective. Before the shooting, she'd been like a preacher's kid, rebelling against the ever-present loom of authority. When her mom died and her dad went off the rails, Beck had reversed course from rebellious teenager to model child, seeking out structure and balance for both Liam and herself. It hadn't been a conscious choice and now she wondered if becoming a cop had been any more of a conscious decision as well.

"I became a cop because I wanted to be like her. She was my hero even if I didn't realize it at the time."

Silence played out between them. She'd overshared, but with her emotions welling up to the surface, she didn't care about holding back.

"Do you want to skip to what happened the night of the shooting?"

Beck was surprised Macy was willing to let her skate through the background info so quickly, but it was kind of like moving from one minefield to another. She shrugged. "You're the interviewer."

Macy set her notebook down and tapped her pencil on the table. "You don't have to do this."

Not the approach she'd expected. "First you talk me into the interview, and now you're talking me out of it?"

"No. I definitely want this story and I think you should be the one to tell it…"

"Then why the reticence?"

Macy met her eyes, but her expression was hard to read, and she didn't have long to try before Macy picked up her notebook again and opened to a fresh page. "Whose decision was it to pull over Mr. Aldridge's car?"

Facts. She could deal with facts, and she rattled them off, curious about why Macy had chosen to have her repeat the testimony she'd given in court the day they'd first met. She didn't dwell on it too long, thankful to ease into her story. When she finally reached the plot twist, she paused.

"Do you want something to drink?"

She laughed. "In a library? You really do have a lot of pull, don't you?"

Macy smiled. "I sneak drinks in. I'm certain Susan knows, but she doesn't ever rat me out."

"Good friend."

"She is." A few beats passed. "Are you ready to tell me how the shooting went down?"

"It was fast. Not faster than the eye can see, but too fast for me to do anything to stop it."

"What would you have done?"

It was an interesting question and one that she'd contemplated many times. If she'd been closer to the action, she could've put herself between Jack and Aldridge. Would Jack have had enough time to change his mind about firing the shots? Would he have tried, or would she have wound up the one dead at the scene and what would have played out after if that were the case?

She'd never know, and it was a waste of time to wonder. "I don't know. I like to think I could've deescalated the situation, but there's no way to know for sure."

"But you saw him fire the shot?"

"Yes."

"And you are certain Aldridge wasn't armed?"

"Yes. Nothing in his hands besides the phone. Nothing in his pockets. Nothing found at the scene that would've resembled a weapon. Jack said he saw a knife, but it must have been a reflection or something else that threw him offtrack."

"Or he didn't see a threat at all. Have you contemplated that possibility?"

"I've contemplated a lot of things."

"Do you let subjects you've arrested get away with those kinds of answers?"

"Not often." She braced for a more specific interrogation, but Macy's phone started making a loud chirping sound.

"Sorry." Macy reached for it and started to switch it off, but she became preoccupied with the screen. "Holy shit. Another one."

Beck tensed. "What?"

"Dead body. White Rock Lake."

Beck wanted to grab the phone out of Macy's hand, take down the details, and head to the scene. But those were the actions of a real detective, not someone relegated to a desk in a warehouse full of dead clues.

Macy slammed her notebook shut and shoved it in her bag. She stood and jammed her chair under the table. "You coming?"

"What?"

"I'm headed to the scene. Do you want a ride or not?"

Beck opened her mouth to tell Macy what a crazy idea that was. That there was no way she could roll up on a crime scene that wasn't hers, let alone with a reporter in tow. But when the words came out, they made perfect sense. "Absolutely. Let's go."

CHAPTER FOURTEEN

Macy snuck a look at Beck who was staring out the passenger's side window, apparently deep in thought. She'd put her ball cap back on, and with her reflective RayBans, she likely thought she was incognito, but Macy would recognize her prominent jawline and flawless skin no matter what. She told herself the attention to detail was her journalism training, but a nagging voice inside whispered her attention to Beck was more than that, and the something else was bordering on perilous. Whatever it was, they'd barely exchanged two words since they'd gotten in the car, and she was afraid to break the spell. She hadn't expected Beck to take her up on her offer to ride along, but she didn't regret asking.

And why not? Nothing about their meeting today was normal. Yes, she'd met subjects at the library in the past—it was a quiet, out-of-the-way place to conduct an interview, but she'd pulled punches in her interview, and she'd never done that before. She'd told herself they hadn't finished their session. That she would have plenty of time to press her points, get Beck to push past her feelings to give real, raw answers to her questions, but she wasn't entirely convinced it was true. She needed to stop treating Beck like she was too delicate to handle tackling tough questions.

After-work traffic was still heavy, but she zipped along side streets, finally reaching the section of the bike trail she was looking for, about four miles from where the last body had been found. She sucked in a breath. As much as she wanted support for her theory the Parks and Rec Killer was back, the idea of another young woman lying dead and bound was abhorrent.

She turned on the road near the trail only to find patrol cars blocking off the road and, unlike on her last visit, no place to park. She circled the area twice and finally settled on the parking lot of a small convenience store not too far away. It would be a hike back to the scene, but a thunderstorm earlier in the day had cooled temperatures to the eighties—a welcome relief from the recent heat wave. She shut off the car and turned to Beck. "Unless you have a special method for getting closer, I think this is as close as we're going to get."

Beck's gaze remained trained on something in the distance. "I don't think I should go with you."

"You don't think you should go at all, or just not with me?"

"Either."

"Suit yourself." Macy turned away and started to walk across the parking lot. She was annoyed she'd asked Beck to join her at the scene and annoyed at herself for ignoring how problematic that might be for both of them. This connection she felt to Beck was problematic, but if she bailed on the profile piece now, she'd have to deal with Jerry and his insistent need to please the board. Besides, who knew how long it would be before she'd be able to get her hands on the cold case files. FOIA requests were all fine and good, but the only one who ever really knew she was getting all that she'd asked for was the one producing the documents and she didn't trust Beck's boss, Mendoza, to comply.

She stopped walking when she reached the first patrol car and willed her brain to focus. She'd deal with the profile on Beck and the cold case files later. Right now, she needed to find out if the body on the trail was another victim of the Parks and Rec Killer, and the best way to do that was to suss out the weakest link among those assigned to guard the scene. She surveyed the group of officers standing over to the side and spotted one a few feet from his colleagues, looking like he was about to throw up. She strode over to him, while keeping a careful eye on the others.

"It's that bad, huh?" she said as she approached him from behind.

"Gross as hell. Wish someone had found this one as quick as the other." He coughed into his hand, stood, and turned to face her, his eyes widening with surprise to find he wasn't talking to a colleague. "Hey, you didn't hear that from me."

"I promise 'gross as hell' won't make it into the paper, but you're going to have to give me something to take its place." She replayed his words. "When you referred to the other, do you mean Jody Nelson?"

"Shit. You're not supposed to be here."

He flicked a glance over at his buddies, but she stepped into his line of sight and waved her hand. "I won't quote you at all, but I need something. Male or female? Age?"

"Macy Moran, since when did you start showing up at crime scenes?"

She turned at the sound of the familiar voice to find Claire Hanlon standing behind her. "Hi, Claire. Just doing my job. I am curious why the squad commander is showing up at crime scenes lately. This one's related to Nelson's death, right?"

Claire grabbed her arm and steered her away from the uniformed officer who sighed with relief at being saved from further interrogation. When they were about ten feet away, Claire faced her with a stern expression. "Seriously, what's going on?"

"I'm a reporter and I'm reporting."

"You taking over for Rob?"

"I'm sure he'll be here any minute. Late as usual. Let's just say I have a special interest in these cases. Kind of like you."

"You should find other interests," Claire said. "We've got enough to do here without you breathing down my neck."

"I'm not going to get in the way, but our readership has a right to know if there's an active serial killer in the area."

Claire snapped. "I need you to stop throwing that kind of language around, right now." She looked around and lowered her voice. "Seriously, Moran. Are you trying to start a panic?"

"You can't blame me for jumping to conclusions when you give me nothing to work with. And you know there's going to be blowback if it gets out you have enough evidence to connect these two cases and you didn't share it with the public."

"You're killing me, Moran."

"Just doing my job. Seriously, can't you give me anything?"

Claire sighed. "Off the record."

"Sure." Macy waited, tense with anticipation. She cared more about getting the information than being able to attribute it to a particular source.

"The victim is female, likely in her twenties. Looks like she was jogging."

"Bound? Strangled?"

Claire sighed. "Bound for sure, but as for the manner of death, the body's been here a few days, so I'll leave that question for the ME."

Macy's mind whirred. If the body had been here a few days, that made the time between Nelson's death and this one less than a week. The Parks and Rec Killer had spaced his victims out over the course of a year. She filed the fact away to be examined more thoroughly later. "How soon on the autopsy?"

"I know you've been stuck in the office for a while, but I'm pretty sure you realize we just found the body. The medical examiner's office isn't even here yet."

"Of course, but I also know you, and I bet you called one of your favorites from the ME's office to show up and they'll rush the report for you. Am I wrong?"

Claire sighed. "Dr. Sophia Reyes is on the way, but we won't have the report for a few days, and it won't be the final version until the tox screens come back weeks from now. You know the drill, so I'm a little confused about why you're asking." She narrowed her eyes. "Why are you here again? I thought you'd graduated out of showing up at crime scenes and slumming it with the rest of us."

"Just trying to keep from getting stuck at the office," Macy said, mimicking Claire's tone. "Anything else you can tell me about the scene?"

"Call me next week. I may know more then."

"Come on, Claire. Give me something to take back."

Claire gestured to the area behind Macy. "You're welcome to talk to the lookie-loos. Whoever did this, might still be hanging around." She jerked her chin. "Maybe it's whoever that is."

Macy followed her line of sight and spotted Beck standing about twenty feet away. Shit. She'd acted too impulsively, bringing Beck along with her. She stared for a moment longer, contemplating how to get her away from here without drawing the attention of the other officers who were stationed nearby. With sunglasses on and her hair stuffed into the ball cap, Beck wasn't likely to be recognized, but if the other officers figured out Beck was here, that would become the story of the day, and Macy needed their focus on this case, not on some meta version of Beck's story.

"She's with me." Macy instantly wished she could reel the words back in, but it was too late. She studied Claire's face, but there wasn't much to see since she had turned back toward the crime scene, having apparently lost interest in the now identified spectator. "I'll leave you to your work. I'll call you tomorrow."

"Next week."

"Sure, whatever," Macy said, tossing the words over her shoulder because she was on the move. When she reached Beck, she grabbed her arm and marched her back toward the main road.

"Easy there," Beck said, shaking off her grip.

"You want easy? Maybe don't show up right when I'm in the middle of talking to one of your so-called brothers in blue."

"Wasn't that Claire Hanlon?"

"It was. See, she's definitely taking a personal interest in these cases."

"She has a reputation for being hands-on, even after being promoted to squad commander." Beck shoved her hands in her pockets. "And don't call these people my brothers in blue. They aren't my family."

"Which I guess begs the question of why you even want to keep your job?"

"I didn't sign up for the force to make friends. I did it to make a difference."

"How's that going for you?" Macy stared at Beck until she finally flinched and looked away. Pushing her might be the wrong thing to do, but she couldn't help it. "Look, I'm sorry to be the one to point this out, but I seriously doubt things are ever going to change for you, but if you really want to make a difference, get me access to those case files and let me do what I'm good at."

"Only if you tell me you have enough for your story, because I don't feel like answering any more invasive questions."

Macy drew a finger across her chest. "Cross my heart. I can make it work."

"Fine. Meet me at Sue's. Eight o'clock, Saturday."

Realizing Beck was done with her for the day, Macy pointed at her car. "I'll be there. You ready to go?"

Beck held up her phone. "I've got a Lyft coming." She pointed down the street. "They'll be here any minute. I should go."

"Sure. Okay. Whatever." Macy was disappointed they wouldn't be sharing a ride back to the library, but she knew it was probably for the best considering her disappointment didn't stem from anything professional. She trudged to her car and slid behind the wheel but didn't start the engine. What she should do was get home and add this latest death to the wall and check in with Unfrozen to see if anyone else was starting to draw the same connections she was. But instead, she sat and watched until an SUV pulled up in front of Beck and whisked her away. Yep. Beck Ramsey was a distraction, but she could hardly wait until tomorrow night. She was in trouble for sure.

CHAPTER FIFTEEN

Beck consulted the list on her phone and checked off each of the case files, ending with the one for Macy's friend, Lauren Webb. The first thing that had stood out while she pulled files from the boxes was the fact that they weren't all grouped together. Macy had acted like it was a known fact the murders had been linked, and if that were true, it wouldn't make sense to file them separately. She didn't need a detective shield to know that much.

You're reading too much into this. Just keep your end of the bargain—no need to go overboard.

Beck shrugged off her inner voice. So far, looking up these cases files was the most interesting thing she'd done since being promoted. For a moment, she flashed back to riding with Macy to the murder scene yesterday. On the drive, she'd been jacked up with the excitement and nervous anticipation of rolling up on a crime scene, and with her shield in her pocket, even more so than ever before. But when they'd arrived, she'd been struck with the disappointment of being stuck waiting in the car because she was neither assigned to the case nor welcome among most of her colleagues. Her disappointment had turned to stubborn resolve, prompting her to leave the car and follow Macy to the scene. It had been a stupid idea. She'd managed not to run into any of the cops gathered there, but she'd seen Detective Hanlon looking in her direction, and she likely would've been discovered had she stayed much longer. Her carelessness could've cost her her future with the department which led her to wonder if she even had a future here—a thought that was both paralyzing and freeing at the same time.

She looked around the room. She might not be able to escape this unit, but there were plenty of cases she could work to solve right here in this room. As long as she kept up with the useless log Mendoza insisted she focus on, she could do whatever she wanted with the rest of the time she was assigned to this outpost. Why not start with the case of the Parks and Rec Killer.

If she was going to really dig into this project, she should probably know a little more about the circumstances surrounding the death of Macy's best friend. She stared at the file. It was thinner than she would've expected after all these years, but she wasn't sure what she expected. The boxes she'd retrieved the files from were covered in dust. It wasn't like someone was dropping in every so often to line the folders with new facts and findings. As much as she hated to admit it, when the Parks and Rec Killer stopped his spree, there'd been some new pressing case, ready to take its place. The media was always ready to move on to the next new thing, which left the officers on the force to choose between focusing their assets on older cases or the shiny new ones and the shiny ones almost always won out.

She turned to her computer and typed Parks and Rec Killer into the search engine. Rows and rows of responses confirmed there had indeed been a serial killer, and at the time anyway, the Dallas police believed the cases lined on the table in front of her were all connected by virtue of being his victims. She scrolled through the first few articles, curious about the news coverage at the time, and found several sensational articles all seemingly designed to spark fear in the hearts of young women who might be inclined to visit the city's parks alone. She lingered over the *Dallas Gazette* articles, checking the byline, but the reporter's name was Wayne not Macy. She wasn't sure why she'd expected to see Macy's name since she knew Macy had only been an intern at the time. Maybe the author's strong voice reminded her of the other articles Macy had written. Maybe it was simply the way most reporters recounted the facts, and she was using her speculation as an excuse to think about Macy.

As if she needed one.

She shrugged off the thought and turned her attention back to the files. The locations were all different, but the manner and means the killer had employed were essentially the same in each case. The victim had been found within fifty feet of the main trail at each location, hog-tied—likely postmortem—and strangled by a length of plain hemp rope that could've been purchased anywhere. The police hadn't recovered any DNA from the scene other than that of the victim and there were no signs of a struggle—no defensive wounds, no skin of the killer under the victim's fingernails. No shoe prints or evidence to indicate a body had been dragged through the dirt. No witnesses, no security camera footage. The only evidence the killer had ever been at the scene was the body he left behind.

She found some notes from one of the detectives indicating they had tried to find a connection between the victims, but other than the fact they were all female and in their early twenties, they didn't have a lot in common. Two college students, a teacher, a hair stylist, and an accountant. She kept reading—a quest to use an objective perspective to find an overlooked clue—and was completely immersed in the reports when a loud bang caused her to jerk to attention.

She looked up to see Mendoza leading a woman into the room and noticed she'd opened the door with such force it had swung into one of the metal shelving units nearby.

"Ramsey, come here," Mendoza said.

She surreptitiously slid a book over the stack of files she'd been reviewing and joined Mendoza and the other woman, who she now recognized as Councilwoman Renee Villa, on the other side of the room. When she reached them, Mendoza smiled, and it struck Beck immediately that something was off since this was the first time she'd seen her sporting something other than a surly look. She glanced at Villa, wondering what power she had to turn Mendoza into a person who smiled.

"Detective Ramsey, this is Councilwoman Villa. She's here to get a tour of our unit. I told her you are logging the files as the first step in digitizing the process, and that you're making excellent progress considering the short time you've been working with us."

Beck waited, but apparently Mendoza's statement was supposed to elicit a response. That the files were going to be digitized was news to her, but it was good news because it would be much easier to locate information if it was electronic, even better if it was tied to a database with keywords, but she sensed Mendoza wasn't interested in her non expert IT knowledge. "Thank you, Sergeant." She held out her hand. "Nice to meet you, Councilwoman. I happen to live in your district."

"I hope that means you only have good things to say about me."

Villa's smile was infectious, and Beck couldn't help but smile back. At least until she caught Mendoza eyeing them suspiciously. Geez, did the woman never ease up? Beck remembered what Mendoza had said on the first day about how none of these cases were solvable, but the mayor's office had taken a special interest, and she also recalled that Villa and the mayor were close allies which probably explained Villa's presence here. She decided to take a risk. "I'd be happy to show you around this room if you like."

"That would be perfect," Villa replied. "Would that be okay with you, Sergeant?" They both turned to look at Mendoza who had plastered on the fake smile again.

"Of course. Whatever you need. The chief said you're to have full access."

Mendoza's words were flat even with the fake smile and Beck wasn't fooled, but if she'd been sent by the mayor, then technically Villa outranked Mendoza and Beck was happy to take orders from someone who appeared to be genuinely interested in providing justice to the victims who were represented in these files.

She spent the next half hour walking Villa through the room of files and answering insightful questions about the way they were stored and the log she was working on. When the questions came about digitizing the files, Beck shot a look at Mendoza who merely shrugged. "I'm pretty new to the unit and haven't been briefed on the next step yet, but I'm sure the plans are already in place."

She wasn't sure of any such thing, but throwing Mendoza under the bus wasn't her style. She immediately thought of Jack and wondered what he would say about that. She shook away the thought. This was different. She didn't know for certain Mendoza was shirking her duty. She might not think much of these cold cases, but that didn't mean she wasn't working them. For all she knew, the hours Mendoza spent in her office with the door shut was a product of her intently reviewing the files and conducting her own investigations.

Probably not, but it wasn't her battle to fight.

Sure it is.

She heard the words in Macy's voice and wanted to brush them off, but she couldn't. Macy was right. These cases were as important as any others. More so because of how much time had passed without any justice for the victims and their families. One more thing she had in common with Macy Moran.

Macy walked through the door at Sue Ellen's and glanced around at the already crowded bar wishing she'd countered Beck's suggestion of the bar as a meeting place. Not that she had anything against bars, obviously, but Sue's was one of the last places she'd seen Lauren alive.

Within five minutes of wandering through the club, the crush of the crowd coupled with the cascade of memories caused her heart to pound and her hands to shake. She hadn't found Beck and she no longer cared enough to stay and risk having a breakdown in front of a bunch of complete strangers. She passed a group of women who gave her strange looks which told her she had only a few moments to make it out before she completely lost it, but as she got close to the door it seemed to recede into the distance making escape elusive. She turned in a panic, desperate to find a way out, and ran smack into Beck's tall frame.

"Hey, I've been looking for you," Beck said, her words sounding slightly muffled like she was underwater. She looked at the door and frowned. "Are you leaving?"

"I can't be here." Macy pushed forward and lunged toward the door, determined not to let anything get in her way. Once outside, she lunged around the corner of the building and leaned forward, putting her hands on her knees, gulping for air. *Breathe. Breathe.*

She had no idea how much time had passed before she was finally able to breathe normally. As she started to stand up, the weight of a hand on her back startled her out of her reverie and she whirled around to find Beck standing behind her wearing a concerned expression.

"Are you okay?"

Damn. She hadn't wanted this at all, let alone in front of Beck. She leaned against the wall and crossed her arms. "Go away."

Beck raised her eyebrows, but she didn't move. "Do I need to call someone? Harrison? Donna?"

"I'm fine." She wasn't, but she didn't need more people to see her losing it. After all these years, she should be able to keep her shit together. What the hell was wrong with her? She continued to take deep breaths. She could do this. She had to do this if she was going to maintain any level of objectivity when it came to her work on this piece. Finally confident she could handle whatever came next, she pushed off from the wall and pointed to the sidewalk. "Are you coming?"

Beck merely nodded and followed her back into the bar. Macy squared her shoulders and pushed through the crowd. A drink was what she needed to dull the buzz, and she headed directly to the downstairs bar. When the bartender approached, she ordered a beer and turned toward Beck who ordered the same.

"Go grab that table," Beck said, "and I'll bring the drinks."

She obeyed, happy to let Beck take charge although she'd never admit it, and she made it across the room just in time to snag the table from a crowd of barely legal kids. She waved at them as they shot her disgruntled looks. "When you're thirty-something, you're going to need to sit down too," she called out as they walked away.

Once the disgruntled kids cleared out, she had a perfect sightline to the bar. She watched Beck pay for the drinks, pick them up, and head her way. She moved through the crowd with confidence, seemingly oblivious to the many heads that turned toward her as she walked by. She couldn't blame the gawkers. Beck was striking and gorgeous and she was riveted and more than a little blown away that all these other people would be left drooling when Beck sat down at her table.

"It's more crowded in here than I thought it would be," Beck said as she set their drinks down and slid into the seat across from Macy.

"It's Friday night."

"When I was young, we started much later than this."

Macy grinned. "Me too. Nowadays, when the clock strikes midnight if I'm not home I turn into a gay pumpkin."

"Is that different than a regular pumpkin?"

"Probably not." Macy took a drink of her beer, hoping they'd moved past her anxiety attack. Her hopes were quickly dashed.

"Are we going to talk about what happened outside?"

"I'd rather not." Macy stared into Beck's eyes, willing her to let it go. "Not right now."

Beck's eyes narrowed a tiny bit, but she didn't look away for a few moments, as if she was trying to read her mind. Finally, she spoke. "Okay."

Macy had been expecting a lot more, but then she remembered to be relieved Beck was willing to let it go. She decided to change the subject rather than examine what was going on in her head. "I turned in my story today."

"The one about me and Jack?"

"That's the one. It'll run in tomorrow's paper."

"Am I going to be upset?" Beck asked.

Interesting question. Macy didn't spend time wondering how the subjects of her pieces reacted. The story was about them in the sense they were the subjects, but it wasn't about them when it came to how it was received. She really didn't care if the people she wrote about were impressed or annoyed with what she wrote because she was merely recording events, not creating them. But for the first time ever, Macy found herself anticipating the reaction of a subject, and the feeling was at once confusing and exciting. She searched for something to say that wouldn't give away her emotions until she'd had a chance to examine them more closely on her own.

"I was fair," she said.

Beck held her gaze for a moment, and then nodded. "I trust that you were."

Silence hung in the air for a moment, and Macy mentally sorted through ways to break it. She wanted to dive in and ask Beck about the files, but she sensed she needed to warm up the subject to keep from spooking her. "How was your day?"

Beck looked surprised at the question. "It was good. Full. I spent a lot of time going through files."

That's it. Macy had to ask. "Did you find anything interesting?"

"Hard to tell." Beck drank from her beer and then set her glass on the table and started fiddling with the coaster. "I did take some time to check out the press coverage of the Parks and Rec Killer from ten years ago. I was kind of surprised not to see your name on any bylines."

"You shouldn't be. I was a senior in college. I was lucky to get to do research or fact-checking for a big story. There were definitely no bylines to be shared with the intern."

"Funny, because when I was reading the articles your paper carried about the Parks and Rec Killer, the voice sounded a lot like the other pieces you've written."

The idea Beck had read enough of her work to detect a voice made her happy, and Macy decided to confide in her. "I interned for the reporter who had the beat at the time. Wayne Paxton. He may have let me write a decent amount of the copy, and that's probably what came across when you read it."

"But only he got the byline?"

"No biggie. That's how it works. Like I said, I was only an intern." Macy considered her next words carefully. "Wayne was a little distracted at the time. His wife had just been diagnosed with cancer—the first diagnosis in a protracted illness. She battled it for years and, during that time, Wayne was torn between digging deep into the story and taking care of her." She took a drink from her beer and started fiddling with the label. "I chipped in. Until Lauren died."

Beck nodded, her eyes full of sympathy. "Too close to be objective?"

"More like too angry to make sense, but something like that."

"But it's okay for you to write about it now?"

Macy replayed Beck's words, but she didn't hear any judgement behind them, only curiosity. "Some might say no, but I would argue I'm the perfect person to write about it because I never gave up on finding the truth. Did Lauren's death affect me deeply? Absolutely. But it's not like I'm at the scene, recounting the facts. The piece I'm working on is a retrospective, an accounting of what happened at the time and what's happened since. I'd argue that with my unique perspective, there is no one more qualified to write this story."

She stopped and stared at Beck, trying to discern whether or not she got it and was rewarded with a slow nod.

"It's like when a cop is shot in the line of duty. Everyone throws in to assist with the investigation and no one rests until the shooter is brought to justice."

"Exactly." Macy slapped her palm on the table for emphasis. "I may not have the answer by the time I'm finished writing, but at the very least the story might spur someone's memory and prod them into coming forward with evidence that can help find the killer." She smiled, happy that Beck finally understood where she was coming from. "And with your help, we may get there so much faster." She leaned forward, arms on the table. "Did you bring the files?"

Beck stared into her eyes for a moment before she answered and Macy held her breath, hoping Beck had not let her down.

"I didn't. I—"

Macy didn't wait for the excuse part of the answer. "Really? We had a deal. Are you telling me you decided I wouldn't mind or notice you changed the terms?"

Beck reached out and put a hand on her arm. The touch was firm and warm and strangely calming. "Are you done?" she asked.

"Depends on whether you're going to say more stupid things."

Beck pointed to her head. "I read the files. All of them. I can tell you exactly what's in them, but removing them without authorization will cost me my job and then I'd be no use to either one of us. Make sense?"

It was Macy's turn to nod slowly. "You have a point, but I don't know you well enough to know how good your memory is."

"Quiz me."

It was a silly suggestion. Or was it? Macy did a mental sort of the facts of the various cases and settled on victim number two. They hadn't talked about her or any of the details of her death, so she could be sure Beck wasn't pulling facts from their conversations. "Tell me the name of the second victim."

"Dawn Michaels," Beck replied without hesitation.

Macy responded with another question. "Where was she found?"

"Samuel Grand Park. It was a Saturday. She'd gone out with her boyfriend the night before, but he hadn't stayed over because he had an early shift at the coffee shop he managed. She went for a run early Saturday morning, and the last person to see her alive was the guy mowing the golf course." She stopped to take a breath and then plunged right back in. "Her body was found in a wooded area, away from the recreational parts of the park. She was bound like the others, and she'd been strangled with a piece of easy to acquire rope." She crossed her arms. "Do you need to hear more?"

"Impressive," Macy said. "But you know what would be even more impressive?"

"What's that?"

"If you told me something I don't already know."

"Is that so?" Beck leaned forward. "You know what would make that a lot easier? Maybe if you weren't so secretive. If you shared what you already know, I'd know where to focus."

Macy sucked in a breath. With Beck so close to her, she was the one who needed some focus, and she struggled to process Beck's words. She was right. It didn't make sense to hold the info she did have so close to her chest at this point, but did she really trust Beck enough to bring her completely in?

Before she could fully comprehend the implications, she opened her mouth and blurted out, "I'll show you mine, if you show me yours."

CHAPTER SIXTEEN

Beck pulled into the driveway behind Macy. She wasn't sure what she'd expected, but it wasn't the large two-story Victorian near Swiss Avenue. Houses in this neighborhood were worth more than Beck expected to make during her entire career as a cop, and she couldn't imagine a reporter, even an award-winning one like Macy, would be able to afford to live here.

Turn off your cop brain.

She tried, but it wasn't an easy task. Her cop brain was the reason she was here, right? If she wasn't here to talk to Macy about the Parks and Rec Killer, then she had no business sitting in her driveway, let alone going inside. Or maybe coming here had felt less fraught with danger than sitting across from Macy at the bar where the buzz of alcohol and the thump of the dance beat served as a siren call, beckoning her to cross the line.

The question was what line and where it was. Or if there was even a line anymore. She'd already crossed a line by talking to a reporter, especially having done so about a fellow cop, and that action alone was likely enough to cement her adversarial relationship with the rest of the force. But the alternative was to sit by and let the media print whatever the hell they wanted, and while silence might have been the more prudent route, she'd already proved silence wasn't her go-to style by speaking out about Jack in the first place.

A knock on the Jeep window startled her out of her thoughts and she turned to see Macy standing beside her door. She rolled down the window.

"Change your mind?" Macy asked.

This was it—a perfect opportunity to decline the invitation, to drive away, and pretend she'd never started working on an unofficial investigation into one of the cases her commanding officer had deemed unsolvable and pretend she hadn't also agreed to come to Macy's house because she was attracted to her allure.

But she was here, and she was curious and what kind of a detective would she be if she walked away now? "Not a chance," she said before she could change her mind.

She followed Macy into the house, noting that Macy locked both deadbolts behind them. The house was even bigger than it appeared from the outside and it appeared to have been frozen in time, furnished with heavy, heritage antique pieces each of which was cluttered with a variety of knickknacks. Again, seemingly out of character with how she'd pictured Macy.

"Is something wrong?"

She met Macy's curious gaze. "Nothing's wrong, but I think I pegged you for more of a minimalist."

"Really?"

"Bad cop instinct, I guess. You always seem so focused on your work, I envisioned you in an apartment with no yard, sleek lines, etc." She gestured toward the room. "This is a lot."

"It was my grandmother's house. She left it to me when she died along with a fund to pay the property taxes for years to come. Otherwise, I'd never be able to afford to live here. The only condition was that I live in the house. If I move out, the house gets sold and the proceeds donated to one of the many charities she donated to when she was still alive. If I stay and have kids, then the house goes to them when I croak. It's a complex legal pain in the ass and could probably be challenged in court, but for a reporter who doesn't make a ton of money, it's the perfect setup." She looked around. "It is a lot. I totally get that."

Beck instantly regretted her insensitivity. "Sorry. I wasn't criticizing. I swear." She drew a finger across her chest. "It's a beautiful house."

"Sure. For a family of ten." Macy gestured toward the hallway. "Would you like a tour?"

"Absolutely." She followed as Macy led her down the hall and pointed out the various rooms. A den, two living rooms, and a giant kitchen. One of the living areas was lined with bookshelves and looked like a cozy bookstore or library nook with leather armchairs and a mid-century style bar cart. Now that she was here, she could almost imagine Macy curled up in one of the chairs, with a heavy glass of whiskey, reading one of the tomes from the giant bookshelves. The image suited her, and she wondered why she ever thought of Macy any other way. What other layers had she missed with her assumptions?

"It's my favorite room."

She turned to see Macy watching her, like this tour was a test of sorts and she was determined to pass. No, she was determined to excel. "I can see why."

"Would you like to see my other favorite room?"

A loaded question for sure, and Beck's mind wandered completely outside professional bounds while she contemplated the more private areas of the house. But it was a little too late to be wondering about boundaries, so she gave the only reasonable answer. "Absolutely."

Macy grinned and pointed down the hall. Beck followed her, noting the creak of the original hardwood with every footfall, giving a slightly spooky feel to the historic house. How many other people had walked these halls? The house was fascinating, but more so was the woman leading her through it. What was it about Macy that had her so intrigued? It could be she was drawn to the similarity of their pursuits. She might not care for the press in general, but Macy was singularly focused on finding the truth. It was the same thing cops were supposed to do, but the difference was Macy did it to sell papers, not for the greater good.

She replayed the thought in her head and realized she sounded like an ass. Plenty of cops she knew got into the work out of a sense of duty, but there were just as many who did it for the stability of a steady paycheck and guaranteed retirement income. They'd put in their twenty, take their pension, and start a new career doing something that was more dream than drudge. Not exactly a higher purpose.

"You get inside your head a lot."

She looked up to see Macy standing at the end of the hallway, staring at her. "I guess I have a lot on my mind."

"Of course you do." She held out a hand.

Beck took her hand and noted the firm grip. Macy tugged her closer and pointed at a closed door.

"Are you ready for a distraction?"

Again, with the infectious grin, and this time, Beck couldn't help but grin back. She had no idea what was in store next but cared more about the contents of this room than the consequences of following Macy inside. As Macy pulled a key and unlocked the door, a flash of anticipation surged through her, leaving a trail of heat in its wake. By the time Macy pushed the door open, she was practically salivating.

Macy reached for her hand again. "Come on in."

The minute Beck crossed the threshold, her mind was blown. She'd completely misread the situation because the room she was standing in wasn't a bedroom, it was a war room. She'd seen similar setups at HQ. Detectives gathered on a task force with multiple whiteboards full of photos and scribbled notes indicating connections between the snips of evidence. She looked around the room looking for the other telltale signs of war, boxes of files, computer monitors, stale coffee, stacks of to-go containers. Check, check, check, and check. Still, her mind was having trouble processing that she was still in Macy's house and hadn't warped back into the homicide unit gathered to solve a crime.

"What do you think?"

She spun in place, drinking in the sensations, but she froze at the sight of a wall plastered with photos and articles and large, block-lettered notes that looked like a graffiti artist had been cut loose on the whole mess. She'd never seen anything like it outside of a TV program and she stood transfixed while she took it in.

"You think I'm crazy, don't you?"

She turned slowly to find Macy staring at her expectantly, like her opinion mattered, which was surprising since Macy didn't strike her as the kind of person who cared what people thought about her. Beck flicked another glance at the wall. It was crazy. An investigation on steroids. But crazy wasn't a value judgment. In fact, she was more than a little impressed by the level of commitment to solving these cases that was present in the room.

"To be perfectly honest, I'm impressed. And a little jealous."

Macy cocked her head. "Jealous?"

"You have the freedom to work these cases in any way you see fit. On the other hand, I have the authority to investigate, but not the permission."

"Permission is for the weak."

"It must be nice to be so cavalier. I've worked hard for my career."

"And you think I haven't? My editor is breathing down my neck for me to put this story to bed and write the kind of clickbait crap that dulls my brain but lines the pockets of our investors. Every day that I focus on this case is a risk that I'll lose this job, but every day, I stand my ground because these stories must be told, not written off as unsolved cases that take up too many resources to be solved."

Beck nodded along with Macy's words. She was right. The stories did deserve to be told, which was why she'd spent the day reviewing the files. She had the intel and Macy had the tenacity. Could they join forces to bring these women justice? And what if Macy's supposition that the killer was back at it was true? Didn't she have a duty to make sure he was caught before he harmed more women?

There's a perfectly capable detective already assigned to the case.

There was, but she doubted Claire Hanlon had a resource like Macy Moran and her Great Wall of evidence. Plus, she knew for a fact Hanlon wasn't spending any time in the cold case unit connecting dots.

Helping Macy solve this case could either save her career or end it—there probably wasn't any in-between. She could hear Liam's voice in her head, telling her to think it through. Talk to her union rep or some other cop she trusted before making the decision to help Macy on the sly, but she already knew that any other officer would tell her to keep her mouth shut and walk away. Of course, they would've said the same thing if she'd asked for advice before reporting her own partner. The bottom line was there wasn't anyone who'd ever been in her situation she could truly trust to guide her in this situation, leaving her to rely on her gut.

She wasn't sure why she was even going through the motions of reviewing the pros and cons since she'd known what she was going to do the minute she walked in this room. *Listen to your gut. Do the right thing.* "Let's find this guy."

Macy hid her surprise at how easily Beck agreed to help with the investigation. She'd expected it would take more convincing and now that she'd agreed, she was kind of at a loss as to where to go next. "Let me show you around."

She pointed at one of the whiteboards across the room, but Beck appeared to be fixated with her wall of facts, and Macy's heart surged as she watched Beck's reaction. No one else had ever been in this room. No one else even knew about it. She kept it locked and carried the key with her always. She wasn't sure what she thought would happen if anyone discovered her research/work in progress, but the idea of sharing this space and its contents had always filled her with dread. The dread of being judged, the dread that came with a lack of understanding. It was easier to keep her pet project secret than to share and risk rejection. It wasn't the rejection she feared but seeing other people's true colors and not being able to unsee them. Yet, instinct had driven her to share this room with Beck, and the captivated look on her face signaled she'd been spot-on.

"This is fascinating," Beck said, raising her hand to point to a group of photos on the wall. "These are all the women, right?"

Macy wanted to beam, but they were talking about dead young women who'd had their lives cut short, so she tempered her happiness that Beck was impressed with her. "Yes. It helps me to have their pictures grouped together. It's a reminder that, other than their relative ages, they didn't have that much in common. They didn't look alike, they didn't dress alike, they weren't all students, and they didn't work in the same professions."

"They were all sporty types—that's why they were all at the lake."

Macy pointed to a photo of a brunette with her hair pulled back. "Not this one. This is Lynn. She may be dressed like she was out for a run, but she was at the lake to scope out a perfect spot for her upcoming engagement photo shoot. Apparently, the arboretum next door charges to reserve space for photo sessions, and she was saving for the big day and was blowing through her budget."

Beck frowned. "None of that is in the police report."

"See!" Macy poked her forefinger into Beck's chest. "This is how we can help each other. I bet I've interviewed more of the parties involved than they did. If I had the full reports and not the half-ass, redacted version they hand out to anyone who asks, then I could fill in blanks here," she pointed to the wall, "not to mention, I'd have a better idea of what information law enforcement doesn't have so I could share with them."

"You know, you could share what you have without conditions."

Macy heard the skepticism in Beck's voice. "You think I'm being an asshole? That if I don't simply hand over my years' worth of work investigating these cases, that I'm obstructing justice or some such?"

Beck raised her palms up. "Hey, don't shoot the messenger. I'm playing devil's advocate here."

"Then try this on for size. I have shared. Every piece of evidence you see on this wall, except for the info that relates to the two recent murders, was provided to the detectives who originally worked this case. Fat lot of good it did. Maybe you should talk to Claire Hanlon about her former mentor, Bruce Kehler. He handled these cases. Or rather, he was assigned to handle them."

She watched Beck's face and caught the exact moment when Beck made the connection. "*Assistant Chief* Bruce Kehler? Damn. I mean I recognized the name. He retired last year."

"Retired implied he had a choice. He was forced out after what happened with Frank Flynn's case," she said. Surely Beck had heard about Flynn having his murder conviction reversed after it was revealed Kehler and his partner had failed to disclose key evidence to Flynn's attorney at trial.

"I heard the rumors."

Macy shook her head. "They were more than rumors. He framed Flynn, and I know for a fact the department combed through every case he had worked on while he was in homicide to make sure there weren't grounds to overturn any more convictions. Plenty of defense attorneys with clients sitting in prison made sure of that." She held up a file. "But I doubt anyone even gave these unsolved cases a second look."

"Holy shit."

"Yep. These files and who knows how many others were buried in the cold case unit with Sergeant Mendoza assigned as the gatekeeper. She does a grade A job of ignoring FOIA requests and keeping secrets buried."

Beck cleared her throat and looked uncomfortable.

"Are you going to stick up for her?" Macy asked, hearing her voice rise, but unable to control her brewing frustration. "Do you think she's even remotely interested in solving any of these cases? If you do, then you need to hand in your shield because you're not going to make it as a detective."

"Hey now," Beck said. "The last thing I want is a reputation for ratting out all of my fellow cops, but I'm not sticking up for Mendoza. I don't know what her agenda is. Hell, I don't know anything about her, but I do know she's not keen on me doing anything but cataloguing case info." She paused for a moment, frowning.

"What is it?" Macy asked, sensing Beck was holding something back.

"Councilwoman Villa came in today. She wanted a full tour of the unit and had a lot of questions about the files. The mayor has assigned her to a task force reviewing the procedures for clearing these cases. If it makes you feel any better, Mendoza seemed pretty annoyed by the visit."

"Her annoyance is a small price to pay for the truth, but I'll take it." She softened her tone. "I appreciate you telling me about Villa's visit. You didn't have to share that."

Beck grinned at her. "We're a team now, right?"

Macy hesitated. It was a big step going from her solitary work behind a locked door, to sharing all the information she'd amassed over the years with someone from the very agency that had kept her shut out from these cases all along. Aside from the amateur investigators at Unfrozen, she'd worked on this case alone, and it was a big step to invite anyone in, let alone a rookie detective. But she needed the help, especially if she was going to wrap up the anniversary piece before Jerry shut her down for good. She had to trust someone. Why not trust a cop who'd shown she had more integrity than most?

She tried not to dwell on the fact that her trust level might've gotten a boost from the blast of attraction she got every time Beck walked in the room. Hell, if she was going to work with someone, it may as well be someone she enjoyed being around, and not simply for her keen mind. She reached for Beck's hand. A simple shake to seal the deal, but when their fingers touched, the surge of arousal took over. Instead of clasping palms, their fingers intertwined, and Macy stepped closer. Beck was a magnet, and she couldn't resist.

The heat was palpable, blazing through her, and judging by the way Beck's eyes went dark, she was feeling it too. Would one quick kiss be enough to extinguish the flame, or would it stoke it into an uncontrollable blaze?

Before she could process the thought, Beck's lips pressed into hers, eliminating the need to analyze. She melted into the taste of her, and the force of their kiss drove away thoughts of conflict and the cases and anything outside of the firm press of their tongues tangled in mutual desire. She lost herself in the pleasure of Beck's sure touch, soft and firm by turns. She moaned with pleasure as every single one of her nerve endings tingled and begged for more. Moments later, when Beck pulled gently back, she was no longer sure where she was or what they'd been doing, and the lack of grounding didn't bother her in the least.

"Are you okay?"

She looked up into Beck's still dark eyes, but she couldn't form the words to convey exactly how much more than okay she was. She reached up and ran her hands through Beck's blond waves, pulling her hair back from her long, sleek neck. She leaned forward and traced a path up the side of her neck with her lips and tongue. Light, teasing kisses, designed to whip Beck into the same kind of frenzy that consumed her. When her lips reached Beck's ear, she whispered, "So much more than okay." She moaned. "So much."

Beck turned in her arms and captured her lips again in a searing kiss, and Macy accepted the invitation. When Beck pulled back slightly to take a breath, Macy laced their fingers together again and with her free hand motioned to the door. "Would you like to see the rest of the house?"

Beck's breath hitched. "Please."

CHAPTER SEVENTEEN

Beck wasn't sure who'd initiated the kiss, but she'd been powerless to stop it. Not that she wanted to. No, stopping wasn't an option. She wanted to lose herself completely in the velvet soft way Macy's lips caressed hers, in the insistent press of her talented tongue. When Macy extended her hand, she had no choice but to follow.

The stairs creaked beneath their feet, but Beck barely noticed as she was swept up in the anticipation of what would be waiting once they climbed to the top. Macy paused when they reached the landing and pulled her back into her arms. She relaxed into her embrace, enjoying the unfamiliar freedom of surrender.

"I have a thing for balconies," Macy murmured against her lips.

Beck looked down at the foyer from their perch. "Balconies are great until someone gets hurt." She used her fingers to mimic someone falling over the edge to illustrate the point.

"Spoken like a true detective. Always suspicious."

Beck leaned back in Macy's arms and scanned her face to determine if she was kidding. "Hey now. If I were always suspicious, I probably wouldn't be here right now."

"Is that so? Do you think I have an ulterior motive in inviting you up here?"

"No," Beck answered quickly, but she immediately questioned her instinct. "I mean you don't, do you? I mean other than…" Had she misread Macy's affection?

"I asked you to come to my house because I wanted to show you how serious I am about these cases, show you what evidence I've already collected." Macy paused and slid an arm around her waist. "But I have to admit, I've been distracted from my mission after seeing you walk through Sue Ellen's like a boss. It's been a while since I hung out there, but I don't recall anyone ever causing that many cases of whiplash simply delivering beers to a table."

Beck felt the heat of a blush creep up her neck, but she was powerless to stop it. Kind of like she was powerless to stop whatever was about to happen between her and Macy. Deciding it was pointless to pretend the only reason she'd agreed to come here tonight was curiosity about the cases, she abandoned any pretense tonight was about duty over desire. She pulled Macy closer. If Macy liked it when she acted like a boss, she could work with that. She leaned down and ran the tip of her tongue along Macy's earlobe, loving the way her breath hitched and she arched into her arms. She whispered, in her most commanding tone. "Take me to your bedroom."

A few stumbles down the hall later, they stopped in front of another door, but this one wasn't locked. Macy pushed open the door and led them into the room and Beck instantly felt like she'd walked into a time machine. The large four-poster bed with its billowing silk canopy was not at all what she would've pictured for Macy, but the second she had the thought she realized how much she'd thought about every aspect of Macy. What her life had been like before she'd met Lauren, and Donna, and Harrison. Before she'd become a reporter. Before Lauren had been killed. In all her thoughts, she'd assumed Macy was tough, having weathered tragedy. She'd assumed Macy's toughness extended to all aspects of her life, and she was ashamed she'd assigned so little depth to this fascinating woman.

"It was my great-grandmother's," Macy said, pointing to the bed. "I bought a new mattress because people in the past must've thought back problems were a badge of honor, but everything else about it is the same."

Beck read the trepidation in her voice. "It's beautiful." She squeezed Macy's hand. "You're beautiful. And complex."

"You say that like it's a good thing."

"And you say that like you believe differently."

Macy shook her head. "Just the facts, ma'am." She leaned back against the wall. "You asked me to bring you here. Did you have something special in mind?"

Beck answered by kissing Macy again, but this time instead of the fast, hungry strokes, she took her time, lingering with each caress, leaning into the slow steady rhythm of their mutual arousal. She could feel the flutter of Macy's heart racing against her chest, and she ached to feel her skin against hers. She slid one hand up and under Macy's blouse, while using the fingers of the other to tug loose the buttons of her shirt.

Hands slid down the front of her jeans, tracing the fly and dipping lower. Teasing touches trailing a path of arousal designed to make her go mad. She thrust her pelvis against the light touch, aching for more strokes, more pressure, more of whatever Macy had to give. Her clothes grew tight and suffocating, and she struggled against them.

Like a mind reader, Macy reached for the buttons on her fly and very deliberately unfastened first one, then another, then another. When she was done, Macy slid her hand into her jeans and began slow strokes in an apparent effort to drive her insane. She braced her hands against the wall behind them and relaxed into the embrace, simultaneously hoping it would last forever and praying for release.

"You're so wet."

"Hard not to be when you're touching me like this," Beck gasped.

"Do you want me to stop?" Macy asked.

"God no, but I can't promise I can stay standing if you do it much longer."

Macy stilled her hand and slowly pulled her fingers from Beck's jeans.

Beck put her hand over Macy's. "Wait. What are you doing?"

"I'm not going to be responsible for you falling and hitting your head." She jerked her chin toward the bed. "How about some righteous cushioning?"

Beck grinned and reached for Macy's hand, letting Macy lead her to the bed. She settled in against the pillows. "I don't know that I've seen this many pillows gathered in one place before."

"I know, right?" Macy nudged her way onto the bed next to her, tracing her fingers along Beck's thigh in a slow, teasing way that drove her to distraction. Macy, on the other hand, didn't seem to notice her growing arousal and continued talking. "I think my grandmother owned stock in Bed, Bath, and Beyond," she said. "Most of the time, I wind up tossing them into that chair over there, but…"

Beck propped herself up on one elbow. "But?"

Macy grinned, arranging the pillows around her. "But I think I just figured out the perfect use for all of this fluff." She placed two soft, squishy ones behind Beck's head and one to her right before leaning down to capture her in another of their slow burn kisses.

"You are the most fantastic kisser," she said when she came up for air.

Macy poked a finger at her chest. "You are." She trailed her finger down the front of Beck's shirt. "The only thing wrong with you is the fact you have too many clothes on right now."

This was it. She was in Macy's bed. She was wet and ready, and she couldn't remember ever having been this aroused. If there was a line to be crossed here, she was ready to vault over it. She placed her hand behind Macy's head and arched up to meet her lips. The kisses before had been hot, but this time their touch was searing, signaling she was ready for more. Much more.

As if she could read her mind, Macy began unbuttoning her shirt and unfastening her bra, her progress excruciatingly slow and painfully exhilarating. Beck's breathing grew labored as she imagined Macy's hands on her skin, and she squirmed against the pillows in anticipation. She had no sense of how long she'd been waiting when Macy finally tugged away her clothes, tossed them to the ground, and fanned her fingers across her stomach, up her chest and began teasing her breasts with slow, raking circles.

"God, you're beautiful," Macy said, biting her bottom lip as she continued to stroke, and pinch, and tease. She bent low. "Tell me what you want."

Beck stared into Macy's eyes, reading the promise of her words reflected in her hopeful expression. There were so many things she wanted in this moment, but she wasn't sure she had the fortitude to form the words with Macy continuing to touch her. One thing. Start with one thing. "Take off your clothes."

Macy's smile grew wide. She kept one hand on her chest and used the other to pull off her T-shirt. "Like this?"

Beck nodded and pointed at her bra. "More, please."

Seconds later, Macy's bra dropped to the floor, and she stepped out of her pants. Beck's breathing grew labored as Macy stood next to the bed, naked, beautiful, and a little bit sassy, with one hand on her hip and the other held against her lips. Beck extended her hand, ready to ask for the next thing.

"Come here."

Macy's eyes grew dark as she stepped closer, and Beck knew she was going to come out of her skin if she had to wait much longer. She reached down and pulled off her jeans and briefs, tossing them to the other side of the bed. She was completely naked now, hungry for the press of Macy's flesh against hers, but when it happened, she was totally unprepared for the shocks that shuddered through her.

"You feel incredible," she murmured, running her hands down Macy's side, curving to cup her ass and press them closer. "I'm so turned on right now."

Macy reached between them and drew her fingers across Beck's sex, her smile widening as she lingered with teasing touches to her inner thighs. "I can tell," she purred. "Let's see how wet we can make you."

Macy stretched up along her torso and began to lick her breasts, with slow, gentle strokes that grew increasingly more intense. Beck writhed beneath her, clutching the bedsheets in her hands while arching into Macy's touch, craving the pleasure of her, and completely oblivious to anything outside of the way her body reacted to each pass of Macy's tongue. Her hips lifted of their accord when Macy moved lower and licked her way down her body to settle between her legs. Macy was a driving storm of fire and desire, and Beck surrendered, wet and ready for her touch. When the orgasm came, it was fierce and sure, and she rode it until every wave subsided and she lay spent in Macy's arms.

Macy tucked up against her, holding her close. "Hey, beautiful," she said, "I hope that was as incredible as it sounded."

Beck choked out a laugh. "I guess I was a little loud."

"'Little' might not be the word I would choose. I think my grandmother heard you from beyond the grave."

Beck reached for one of the pillows and smacked Macy lightly on the head. "You're hilarious. Besides, it's all your fault."

"Tell me more."

Beck smiled at Macy's eager face, as she replayed the night so far. She had been loud, and she wasn't ashamed of exclaiming about the best orgasm of her life. But the thing she really dwelled on was the fact she'd been so consumed with how Macy made her feel, she'd managed to shelve her ever vigilant cop brain and tune out everything else around her. That had never happened. Ever.

Tonight, she chose to believe it was a good thing.

Macy rolled over in bed and grabbed one of the many pillows that lined the other side of the bed, but instead of squishing in her fist, the pillow moved against her grip. Her eyes shot open to find the pillow wasn't a pillow at all, but instead the very tousled, very sexy Beck Ramsey, lying naked in her bed. A cascade of memories made the night before flooded her brain and she closed her eyes again and let them replay in slow motion. Best. Sex. Of her life. Without question.

Any other weekend morning, she would've been awake already for several hours. Coffee first, then the paper, then she'd unlock her study and sign on to Unfrozen and begin a fresh scan of all the posts, hunting for clues. It was her life. It was fulfilling. It was the most important thing she could do to honor Lauren's memory. Yet here she was on Sunday morning, exhausted and sated after a night of sex with a beautiful woman, and torn between routine and refreshingly new. Routine was losing this battle.

"What are you thinking right now?"

She looked down at Beck and wondered how long she'd been awake, staring at her, and exactly what she'd been able to discern from her expression. "Just reliving the past ten hours." She breathed deep. "You're pretty incredible."

Beck reached for her hand and entwined their fingers. "Said the truly incredible one." She sighed. "I don't think I can sit up, let alone walk." She scooted closer and kissed Macy's shoulder. "But I don't need to do either of those things if we stay right here all day."

All day. All day meant the soonest she could get to her study to sign on would be tonight. Maybe she could offer to make coffee and do a quick check-in right now. She stared at Beck's gorgeous body, her exposed skin. She didn't want her to leave, and she didn't want to leave her either. Her mind raced, looking for a way to have all the things she wanted at once, praying this wasn't a zero-sum game.

"Or I could go…" Beck said hesitantly.

Macy met her eyes and instantly regretted the question in them and the fact she'd left her wondering. "No. I don't want you to go."

"I hear a 'but.'"

She wasn't going to be able to get much past Beck, so why was she even trying? "I want to stay here in bed with you. And I want coffee. And I need to read the paper. And check in downstairs. And speaking of the paper, your profile piece comes out today."

"It's your profile piece, not mine. I'm merely the subject."

Macy tucked into Beck's arms and fanned her fingers out on her chest, and the feel of Beck's warm skin under her hands sent heat coursing through her. "There's nothing 'merely' about it. Though it's a good thing last night didn't happen before I turned in the piece or I'm pretty sure everyone who reads it would figure out I have a personal bias."

Beck sat up and leaned back against one of the many pillows. "This is what we're going to do." She ticked the items off on her fingers. "First, we get coffee. Second, we read the paper. And third, we go down to your war room and start filling in blanks. You may have forgotten in all the kissing, that I've reviewed the department files on each case. If there's something missing from what you have, chances are good I'll be able to tell you."

Macy stared at Beck, barely able to process what she'd just heard. Was she really willing to spend their morning-after going over cold case evidence? If so, she was a dream come true, and she should take advantage right freaking now before she changed her mind. But the mention of kissing caused her to pause and adjust. "I have a slightly different plan. First, we do a bit more of this," she slid her hand up Beck's naked thigh, letting it come to a rest, inches from her sex, "and then the rest."

Beck answered by tossing off the sheets and rolling over so she was on top. Macy scooted back against the mountain of pillows, unsure who she even was right now because the call of the evidence in her study wasn't nearly as strong as the thrum of her body at the anticipation of Beck's touch. She told herself she wouldn't allow her personal pleasure to overtake her professional mission, but the moment Beck closed her lips over her breast, her promise faded, and she surrendered completely to the sensations of pleasure.

❖

Pleasantly delayed by a couple of hours, Macy made them each a cup of coffee, gathered the paper from the front porch, and led the way to the war room. She liked that Beck called it that because after ten years of battling to gather bits of information, she felt as if she'd been engaged in an epic war, and with the possibility of the killer being back in action, the climax seemed near.

The first thing she noticed when they entered the room was the flashing alert on her main computer screen, letting her know she had new messages from Unfrozen. She shot a look at Beck who was standing in front of the wall with her hands on her hips and made a snap decision. "Hey, do you mind reading the article while I check my email? I'll be able to focus a hell of a lot better if I'm not wondering what you think about it while we work."

Beck looked surprised at the ask. "Sure, but how about we agree not to let it come between us, no matter what?"

"Fine by me." Macy had been telling the truth about the dread of being in the same room with the subject of her piece, which was another odd thing about the last twenty-four hours because it was not like her to care what anyone else thought about the way she chose to tell the stories she wrote. That she cared now, with Beck, signaled she needed to tread carefully in this relationship, both personally and professionally, but right now she was too anxious to get to her messages to dwell on it.

When Beck was safely settled across the room, she pulled up the link to Unfrozen and signed in. The first message waiting for her was from Huntsman363.

Any news?

Well, that was deflating. She'd hoped for some new clue she could develop, but maybe Huntsman was using one of her tactics, holding facts close until a higher level of trust was developed. She typed a quick response.

Nothing definitive. Opinions?

A few moments passed, and she was beginning to wonder if he'd already signed off, when Beck called out from across the room.

"I'm only halfway in, but I have to say I expected you to be a bit harder on me. I mean, especially after the last piece where you implied I should've known about Jack's propensity for anger and should've reported it sooner."

Macy tore her eyes away from the screen long enough to say, "You better read the rest of it before you let me off the hook."

"Uh-oh." Beck grinned. "I'll report back in a just a few."

Macy barely heard the words as the screen in front of her flashed with Huntsman's response.

I think it might be a cop.

She stared at the screen, transfixed. She'd had the same thought. Lots of times. It would explain so much about why the cases had never been solved. The lack of any significant forensic evidence. The ability to lure young women off the park trails. And it wouldn't be the first time a serial killer had law enforcement experience or aspirations. The Golden State Killer sprang to mind, along with Dennis "BTK" Rader and "Coed Killer" Edmund Kemper. Even the infamous John Wayne Gacy had pretended to be a cop to pick up his victims.

And it would explain why Claire Hanlon, a squad commander, was personally handling the recent cases. Cases that would normally be assigned to a detective under her command. Macy hunched over the keyboard, poised to reply, when Beck's voice startled her out of her thoughts.

"I finished it."

She looked up to see Beck walking toward her. She was steps from her now, too far away to see the screen, but in a second that would change. *I think it might be a cop.* Macy kept her eyes on Beck while she reached up and hit the escape button on her keyboard, watching the Unfrozen screen disappear from the corner of her eye before Beck was at her side. She breathed a sigh of relief, crossed her arms in front of her chest, and gave Beck her full attention.

"What did you think?" she asked, still surprised to find she really wanted to know.

"It was fair. You didn't make me out to be a hero, which I'm not. It was way more stick to the facts than a lot of your feature pieces."

Macy smiled. "I may have gone a little overboard with the whole trying to stay objective when I'm really not."

"I'm cool with that," Beck said, her slow, easy smile signaling she might be thinking of last night too. "I'm sure it won't make much difference to the rest of the force, but I like the idea of having my side of the story out in the world."

"You didn't do anything wrong."

"I know, but there are hundreds of folks on the force who don't know me well enough to judge." She held up the paper. "Maybe a few will be able to set aside their prejudice and cut me a break after reading this. Thank you."

"Just reporting the facts. I told you I wouldn't sugarcoat things." Macy flicked a glance back at her computer screen to make sure it hadn't mysteriously come to life.

I think it might a cop.

What would Beck say if she shared that theory with her? Would she agree from her position to the left of the thin blue line, or would she reflexively side with her brethren because she aspired to be part of the group again someday? An image of Beck, sexy, affectionate, attentive, flashed in her mind. Testing her will.

She dug in. No matter what had happened between them last night, no matter how much she thought she knew about Beck, she couldn't be entirely sure how Beck would react to this theory. And until she was, she wasn't about to take a risk that might tank her life's work. No matter how much she wanted to.

CHAPTER EIGHTEEN

Beck pulled up in front of her apartment building and sat for a moment in her Jeep while she wrapped her mind around the idea of moving back into her place. She was tired, but it was a good tired, and she tried not to dwell on the abrupt end to her time with Macy. She had work to do. When she was no longer riding a desk, she'd have a higher likelihood of being called away at a moment's notice too. The best thing she could do right now was be the understanding girlfriend.

Girlfriend. She hadn't caught the thought in time to stop it, but now that she'd used the word, she rolled it around in her brain to see how it fit. And it fit nicely. She'd enjoyed waking up in Macy's bed, sharing coffee and the paper while discussing their mutual work.

Careful. You barely know her.

It was true. She didn't know Macy well, but she'd always trusted her instincts and right now they told her that Macy was a good person. And her body told her she was a magnificent lover.

A knock on her window interrupted her thoughts, and she turned to see Alicia Staples, Jack's wife, standing outside next to the Jeep. What the hell?

She motioned for her to step back, and she climbed out of the car and looked around, half expecting to see Jack nearby.

"He's not here," Alicia said. "It's just me."

"Alicia, you shouldn't be here," Beck said.

"Are you saying you won't talk to me?"

Beck glanced around, though she wasn't sure what she expected to see. A reporter, looking to get a follow-up to Macy's story? Someone from internal affairs, wondering why she was talking to Jack's wife? All she saw were people enjoying their Sunday afternoon. Walking their dogs, jogging, playing tennis. The world turned at its usual speed despite whatever was going on with her, and the sooner she realized it, the better off she'd be. Still, she didn't want to have this conversation—whatever it might be about—standing in the parking lot of her apartment.

"I'll talk to you, but not here." She shut the door to the Jeep and locked it. "Come on."

Once they were inside her apartment, she invited Alicia to have a seat and told her she'd be right back. In her bedroom, she looked at herself in the mirror, surprised to see she looked fairly put together despite the fact she was wearing yesterday's clothes and she'd had barely any sleep.

She smiled at the memory of waking up in Macy's bed. At the way Macy was torn between her work and their affection, and that they'd found a way to combine the two. They'd ordered in breakfast tacos and pored over the case files all morning until Macy had gotten a call from her editor with a time sensitive assignment. The last twenty-four hours had been the most fun she'd had in a very long time, and she was already thinking about when she could see Macy again. All she wanted to do right now was take a nap and slip back into the memory of last night.

But Jack's wife was sitting in her living room, and she needed to deal with her before she could do anything else. She pulled her hair back, washed her face, and changed into a pair of shorts and her favorite UT T-shirt, and walked back out into the living room, determined to deal with whatever Alicia wanted in short fashion. But when she saw her huddled on the couch, her eyes dark and swollen, her resolve faded.

"Can I get you something to drink?" she asked, seizing on the simple task as a way of avoiding whatever Alicia had to say.

"No. I just want to talk to you," Alicia said, her voice strong and sure in spite of her appearance. "I won't keep you long. I promise."

Beck sat down in the chair across from the couch. "Okay. I'm ready."

"I know Jack better than you."

Beck waited for a follow-up to the declaration, but a few seconds passed with only silence between them. "Is that a question? What do you want me to say?"

Alicia cleared her throat and shook her head. "I don't know. I'm at a loss here. Jack has a temper. I know this. Anyone who knows him knows it's true, but I've never seen him hurt anyone. He's never laid a hand on me, or our kids." She reached in her pocket and pulled out a Kleenex, dabbing it at the corner of her eyes. "I don't understand how he wound up in this situation."

Alicia looked up and stared directly at her. "If you were to tell them you made a mistake, this would all go away. You have that power. Why won't you use it?" She wrung her hands. "He was your partner, your friend."

It was a gut punch. Yes, she'd always considered Jack a friend, but through the lens of retrospection, she wasn't sure that had ever been true. Stuck in a car together, day after day, they'd talked and joked and shared light confidences, but all of that had been more about adapting to the environment than genuine affection. She cared more about Macy Moran who she'd known for less than a month than she did about Jack or the rest of his family, especially since he was the one who put her in this position.

She did care about him. It would be almost impossible to share such a big part of her life with someone and feel nothing, but she wasn't interested in being dragged into his drama any more than she already was. She met Alicia's eyes and wondered what her life with Jack was like. Was she here because she really cared about him or was she merely trying to salvage any normalcy she and her kids had left?

"What do you want me to do?"

"What I said. Tell the prosecutor you made a mistake. That you didn't have a good angle to see. That you were caught up in the circumstance, afraid of being shot yourself."

Beck sighed. "You want me to lie."

"Can you not even entertain the idea you might be wrong, or are you so locked into your version of events and the notoriety it gives you that you can't bear to tell the truth now?"

"What the hell?"

"I read the paper this morning. You're the big feature story. I can't believe you talked to the press when you won't even talk to Jack."

Beck started to say it was Jack who wouldn't talk to her. Jack who'd told his buddies to haze her for speaking the truth. But Alicia wouldn't, couldn't know all of that. Jack would have shielded her from the truth.

She'd spent so many hours with Jack. In the car. At his house for barbecue, drinking beer, shooting hoops. Except for the times they were on patrol, Alicia had been there for a lot of it, but it was as if she didn't know her at all. She'd allowed herself to think Jack and Alicia were like family, but they were nothing like Liam, who might question her judgment, but would never question her integrity.

"Alicia, don't you think I've gone over every detail of that night hundreds of times? Every second is burned into my brain. Not because I've been asked to recite it or gave an interview to the paper, but because I saw it happen. In real time. Right in front of me. We never should've pulled Ben Aldridge over in the first place, and believe me when I'm telling you that Jack shot him for no reason whatsoever. I will go to my grave believing that was true."

Beck delivered the words with force, hoping they would convince Alicia to leave her alone, but she was completely unprepared for her to burst into tears. She shifted in her seat, unsure how to deal with the messy display, finally springing from the chair to go in search of Kleenex. She brought them back and handed Alicia the box.

"I'm sorry," she sobbed. "This keeps happening. I think I have it together, and then I realize our lives have fallen apart. He was so kind and gentle when we met, but the longer he's on the force, the angrier he gets. I don't think he even likes being a cop anymore, but there's nothing I can say to make it better. And now..." She shook her head. "Now, I don't know what to do."

Beck's heart ached for her. Alicia hadn't asked for any of this. She might have known Jack wasn't right, but how was she supposed to know what to do about it when even she didn't know, and she'd served by his side for years. Summoning all the compassion she could find, she reached for Alicia's hands and squeezed gently. "He needs to take a deal. If he goes to trial, he's going to go to prison for a long time."

"He won't ever agree to plead guilty."

"I know it will be hard for him, but it's the best thing for your family. A trial will be as painful for you as it is for him. And think about Jack Jr. Put this behind you and find a fresh start. It could take a year before he goes to trial. Do you really want to endure the frenzy of attention from now until then?"

Alicia wiped away the last of her tears and abruptly stood. "I should go. I'm sorry I bothered you."

Beck wanted to protest, tell her they could talk some more, but the words didn't come. She didn't really want to talk about Jack's case. Not with anyone on the other side of it, anyway. Alicia would do whatever she wanted to do, and she had no control over the outcome. All she could do was tell her truth.

After Alicia left, Beck's first instinct was to pick up the phone and call Macy. Tell her what had just happened, not like a tipster giving her the news, but like a friend who needed to vent, to decompress. Except they were more than friends now. What she really wanted to do was shower and then go back over to Macy's and repeat the last day, but when she replayed the thought in her head, she remembered how focused Macy was on her work and the better thing to do was to give her that space. That's what friends would do. The real question was what would a lover do?

CHAPTER NINETEEN

Macy walked through the newsroom, determined that this was going to be a perfect Monday. A perfect week on the heels of a perfect weekend. She'd woken up to a *good morning, miss you* text from Beck and *a nice profile piece* text from Wayne, and she was ready to tackle anything that came her way.

Within moments, her determination was dashed. Jerry was sitting in her office waiting for her and he wasn't alone. Macy stood in her doorway, taking a moment to size up the suit taking up one of her chairs.

"Morning, Macy," Jerry said. He gestured to the guy next to him. "This is Holt Baxter from the Baxter Group. They're considering an investment in the paper and Holt wanted to meet our star player."

He kept his face slightly turned away from Holt as he spoke and she read the desperation in his expression, begging her to be nice and play along because he didn't have a choice. Which meant she probably didn't have a choice either if she wanted to keep her job. She mustered some of the joy she'd felt before she walked in and stuck out her hand. "Macy Moran, nice to meet you."

Holt gave her hand a firm grip and flashed a super white smile. "Pleasure is all mine."

He motioned for her to take a seat and she resisted pointing out it was her office after all. For now, anyway. She settled in and leaned back in her chair. "What can I do for you?"

Holt shot Jerry a look and turned his charm her way. "I read your piece yesterday about the cop who ratted out her partner. Good work."

She started to correct him, tell him Beck was much more than a few word sound bite, but there wasn't any point. She'd read plenty about the Baxter Group. They bought up papers and turned them into blogs, digital zines. If the Baxter Group bought the paper her future would be elsewhere, which gave her little motivation to be nice, but then she thought about Jerry and how he was nearing retirement and wouldn't be able to find a job in the current market with what most viewed as dinosaur skills. She mustered all the charm she could summon.

"Thanks. I do my best."

"I was thinking about that," Holt said, leaning forward with his arms on her desk. "What if you did a tandem piece? Interview that chick's partner. The shooter. I hear he hasn't given an interview to anyone."

Holy shit, she needed to shut this down. She looked at Jerry who shrugged just before Holt turned to him and said, "What about it, Silva?"

"I definitely think there's an angle there. I'll go over it with Macy and we'll get back to you with our plan soon."

"Make it by the end of the week." Holt stood and looked at his watch. "Have to go. Board meeting in five." He waved at Macy. "Can't wait to read the piece on Staples. You've got promise."

He left so fast Macy didn't have time to chunk her stapler at him. Instead, she turned to Holt's accomplice. "What the hell, Jerry?"

He shrugged again. "What do you want me to do? The guy's got a point. It may seem a little Geraldo Rivera, but telling both sides of a story is one of the objects of journalism. Right?"

"Wrong." She shook her head. "I mean not always right. I write with a point of view. I already gave you the profile on B—" She paused for a second. "Ramsey. I'm not interested in seeing the other side. You want a profile, get Rob to do it."

"Rob sucks at anything other than a few paragraphs covering the five Ws. You're the right person for this story."

She did a mental checklist of all the reasons her authoring a profile piece on Jack Staples was a bad idea, but the one reason that flashed the biggest warning sign was the fact she'd slept with the subject of the opposing piece, and she wasn't about to tell Jerry that. What she needed was time. If she could put him off long enough, something else might come up. Or maybe she could finish her feature on the Parks and Rec Killer and leverage that into getting out of this insane assignment. Bottom line, she wasn't writing a story about Jack Staples. Not of her own free will.

After Jerry left her office, she turned her attention to the pieces of evidence Beck had filled in. Unfortunately, there wasn't a ton, but the lack of evidence tended to bolster her burgeoning theory that the killer might be a cop who either knew enough to cover his tracks at the scene or had access to be able to hide evidence and alter reports. She wanted to share her idea with someone, and a couple of times, she reached for the phone to call Beck, but discarded the idea before she punched the numbers. Beck might be on the outside now, but she was still committed to her career in law enforcement. After everything she'd gone through since Jack's arrest, would she be likely to embrace the idea of another officer gone bad, let alone help take him down?

She did the right thing with Jack.

Macy acknowledged it was true, but if she cared about Beck, why should she put her in the position of having to?

And she did care about Beck. She scrolled past Beck's number and scanned the list of contacts in her phone. Harrison and Donna were full up from hearing her theories, and she'd have to bring them up to speed on everything that was going on at the paper before they'd even get her dilemma. If she called either one of them, they would encourage her to take a break from her work, go on vacation, and try to find some balance in her life. Not helpful. She kept scrolling, about to give up when her thumb stopped on

Wayne's number. He'd already read the profile on Beck and would understand exactly what she was going through.

I could use a sounding board. Free for lunch?

She pressed send before she could give it another thought. His response was almost immediately.

Sure. Someplace downtown?

She'd been about to suggest they meet someplace up north since he lived in Plano now, but downtown was better for her. Thinking she should treat him to someplace nice since she was about to pick his brain, she typed *Capital Grille?*

Too fancy.

Ah, I know the perfect place. Meet me by the fountain at Kyle Warren. 11:30.

She stayed in her office with the door shut until it was time to meet Wayne, and when she left, she took the back door to the stairs, hoping to avoid any sightings of Holt Baxter because if she saw him, she wouldn't be able to resist the temptation to punch him in the face. She used the time walking to the park to contemplate her options. She wanted the paper's platform to promote her piece on the anniversary of the Parks and Rec Killer, but not at the expense of having to write stories she couldn't stomach. And she wouldn't be able to stomach writing Jack Staples's side of anything even if she wasn't personally involved with Beck. The guy had killed an innocent civilian in cold blood. He didn't deserve a platform to justify his crime.

There was a time, when she'd just started her career, she would've jumped at the chance to cover any angle, and truly believed her job as a reporter was to tell all sides of a story, but after all the good and bad she'd seen over the course of her career, she no longer believed true objectivity was possible or was even warranted. Besides, if she did agree to interview Jack, it wasn't like she was going to be reporting pure facts, only his version of them.

But you were perfectly willing to showcase Beck's side of the story.

True. Of course, she'd had something to gain by doing it, but at the heart of it, she didn't balk at telling Beck's side because she believed it to be true, and she'd held that belief long before she'd gotten to know her. Which brought her back to the original point. She might be a reporter, but she was also a person with personal opinions, and trying to pretend those didn't inform her work was ridiculous.

"You're early."

She turned to find Wayne standing right behind her. She must've been too lost in thought to see him there, but now that he was here, she was thankful she'd have someone to talk to about her dilemma who would get why she was conflicted. "I rushed to get out of the office. Let's grab some food and I'll tell you all about it."

They grabbed falafel wraps from one of the food trucks and settled in at one of the tables in the park. "Talk or eat first?" Wayne asked.

She stared at the wrap and decided food would go down easier if she got what was bugging her off her plate. "Talk, unless you're starving." He shook his head and she continued. "First, thank you for your text about the Beck Ramsey profile," she said, noting the weirdness of using Beck's name, considering they were long past being on a first-name basis.

"I meant it. You do good work." He cocked his head. "I sense you didn't invite me here to thank me. What's on your mind?"

She appreciated the way he went straight to the point. "Jerry wants me to do a tandem story on Beck's former partner, Jack Staples."

"Ah, I see."

"Right?" It was such a relief to talk to someone who got the situation. "Of course, Jerry doesn't know I had an agreement with Beck that I would tell her side of the story and she would help me on the anniversary piece."

"You certainly did your part. Did you get what you wanted from her in return?"

What a loaded question. "Yes. We met over the weekend, and she filled in a bunch of blanks from the police reports that have been held hostage all these years. Frankly, there wasn't a lot to fill in when it comes to actual information, but I did get some insight into what a crappy job the cops did on the initial investigation."

"Like?"

"According to Beck, they didn't even have the files grouped together. It was like they weren't ready to commit to the idea there was one killer, or they didn't think it was important to try to draw connections. And to be honest, they didn't appear to dig very deep on any of these cases. You were reporting on the cases at the time. Were the cops resistant to the idea these women were all killed by the same person? I mean, I know they weren't fond of the moniker, but surely they didn't think it was a coincidence these women all died under the same circumstances."

He looked surprised to be asked the question. "No, no. There were a few detractors who thought some of the killings were done by a copycat, but the consensus was all the girls were killed by the same person." He looked up at the sky like he was trying to recall pertinent facts. "I remember speaking to the lead detective."

"Bruce Kehler?"

He shook his forefinger. "Yes, that's the one. He said there wasn't a lot to go on. The killer was very careful. No DNA, no fingerprints, no footprints. He said they were at a dead end."

"Of course he did."

"What are you implying?"

She hadn't meant to say the words out loud, but now that she had, it was the perfect time to test her theory with someone who was well skilled in critical thinking. Someone other than Beck, who might have a personal bias. "I think the killer was a cop."

He nodded his head slowly, like he was wrapping his head around the idea. "Interesting. Do you have anything concrete to go on?"

"Not really. It's more of a gut feeling. But Claire Hanlon, a squad commander, is handling the recent cases personally. And she used to be Bruce Kehler's protege—before he went down for the way he'd handled the Frank Flynn case. You may have heard about that one since it made national headlines."

"I did," he said. "Do you think Hanlon's trying to cover something up?"

Macy had given the matter hours of thought, but she still wasn't sure where she came down on the subject. "I guess it's possible, but it's equally possible she's heading up the current investigation because they suspect Kehler might be involved, and she probably knows him better than anyone else." She shook her head. "I'm not sure which of those is most plausible."

"What does your pal Beck think about your theory?"

Macy hesitated for a second before admitting she hadn't told her.

"She might have a gut feel," Wayne said. "Do you think she can be trusted?"

So many loaded questions today. She trusted Beck enough to show her everything in her study. Well, almost everything—she'd avoided letting her see the threads from Unfrozen, but it wasn't like she couldn't access those on her own. And she'd trusted her enough to share her bed and the most amazing night of sex she'd ever had, but that had only made it more complicated to let her in on her theory. It was complicating everything since it was the reason she couldn't tell Jerry exactly why she wouldn't do the story on Staples, and maybe if she could tell someone about it, she could relieve some of the pressure and see a path forward.

"I slept with her." Once she blurted out the words, she couldn't stop. "She's insanely attractive, and smart, and funny. I'd already turned in the profile piece before it happened, but I won't lie—I thought about sleeping with her way before I'd finished writing it."

"Did you slant the story based on how you felt about her personally?"

It was a fair question, and she took her time to carefully consider her answer. "No. I mean, I believe she's telling the truth about what happened with her partner, but I believed that based on the initial coverage of the case before I was ever involved. I didn't write that piece on her with the idea of currying favor. I swear."

He laughed. "You don't have to convince me." His expression morphed into serious mentor mode. "A good journalist does their best work when it's personal. That's true for you and everyone else. Objectivity implies a lack of concern, but caring about an issue, a consequence, a person will motivate you to dig deeper and never settle for the easy answer. Consider talking to her. If she's as smart as you say, she may have the same gut feeling and can help point you in the right direction."

She took his words in, rolling them around in her head for a moment before deciding he was probably right. There was no denying she had feelings for Beck, but they wouldn't be worth pursuing if she didn't trust her enough to consider all the possibilities when it came to the Parks and Rec Killer's identity. She had one more person she wanted to talk to in order to try to confirm her theory, and then she'd share it with Beck. If there was any fallout, she'd deal with it. No, *they* would deal with it. Together.

CHAPTER TWENTY

Beck looked back over her shoulder to make sure the file room door was still shut and logged in to the department's online file system to look up the case files for the recent White Rock Lake murders. She'd been wanting to do this all week, but Mendoza had been on top of her with a list of information Councilwoman Villa wanted to see for her cold case task force.

She wondered what Villa would think of her clandestine mission to help Macy solve the Parks and Rec Killer cases, and decided she'd probably be all for it based on the way she was sending Mendoza scurrying around like a total boss. According to Foster, Mendoza was on her way to Villa's office, which meant this was the perfect opportunity for her to sign on and check the status of the current cases. She pulled out her phone and started taking notes. Victim one was Jody Nelson, college student. She'd been biking on the trail around the lake. She'd never forget this one since she'd responded to the call that a body had been found. While she'd been tasked with the busy work of securing the scene, she'd seen Jody's body up close, and the image of her, bound and strangled, was burned in her mind.

Claire Hanlon and her squad had conducted extensive interviews of Jody's friends and family, but they'd come up empty. Jody didn't have any known enemies. She biked often at the lake, but she didn't follow any regular routine, sometimes cycling in the morning and sometimes at night. The primary difference between her case and the ones committed by the Parks and Rec Killer was there was a sign of a scuffle at the scene, but the killer hadn't left behind any forensic evidence. Whoever committed this crime had likely convinced Jody to follow him off the trail, but at some point, she'd realized she was in danger and tried to escape. If only she'd been able to scratch him or pull his hair, they might've been able to recover some DNA, but the ME's report showed no evidence from any defensive wounds or Jody's clothing.

The second victim had been harder to identify because it had been several days before she was discovered, but dental records revealed her to be Marisol Garza. Marisol had just graduated from the law school at Richards University, whereas Jody was an undergrad, and she was spending her days studying for the bar exam in July. At twenty-five, she was older than Jody and the past victims, and according to her friends and family, she was only a sporadic jogger who mainly exercised when she was stressed. Based on information Claire's team had been able to put together, they believed she'd gone to the lake several evenings before she'd been found after a particularly grueling day of studying. The primary differences between this crime scene and the others were that the body was located farther from the main trails, there were unmistakable signs of a scuffle, and the ME had found traces of DNA under Marisol's fingernails that was not her own.

Jackpot.

Except they hadn't been able to trace it to anyone in the system yet. Beck read further and found a note from Claire requesting one of the detectives assigned to the case open an account with one of the over-the-counter DNA services to see if they could track the specimen that way, but that could take months and still come up short.

She stared at the screen for a moment, trying to figure out if there was some clue right in front of her she wasn't catching, and was lost in thought when she heard the rattle of the door handle across the room. She reached up to sign out of the system, but stopped and grabbed her phone, taking quick screenshots of the information on the screen before she shut it down just in time to hear the door open into the room.

"I'm headed out," Foster called out. "Sergeant Mendoza is on her way back. You need anything?"

She needed a lot of things, but none that she could openly request. Deciding it would be a good idea for her to be gone when Mendoza got back, she asked him to wait for her.

"Got a hot date?" he asked when she joined him up front.

"Maybe." She and Macy hadn't spoken much this week aside from texts back and forth, but what she'd learned about Marisol's case was worthy of an in-person visit.

"Well, have fun." He held open the door for her. "Wish me luck. I've got a doctor appointment in the morning, and I think I'm finally getting cleared to get back in the field."

"That's great." She was happy for him but disappointed at the idea of having to deal with Mendoza on a daily basis without him as a buffer. Maybe if she helped solve these cases, she might get reassigned. But then she remembered that her assignment here had had nothing to do with her skill and her optimism started to fade. *It's only temporary. It's only temporary.* She repeated the mantra the next few miles, and at the next stoplight she texted Macy, asking if she could come by her place. The response was so quick and enthusiastic, her optimism was instantly restored. She'd take this information to Macy's, and they'd sort through it together.

Macy was standing on the front porch when she arrived, holding two bottles of beer and wearing a big smile. She handed one of the bottles to Beck. "I don't know about you, but I've had a really shitty week so far, but seeing you walk up these steps makes it all okay."

Beck tilted her bottle toward Macy's. "Cheers to that."

Macy pointed to the door. "Okay if we take this inside? As much as I love the charm of a big front porch, it's too damn hot out here."

"Agreed." Beck followed her into the house. The first thing she did when she walked across the threshold was stare up at the balcony, and memories of last Saturday night flooded her mind.

She had no idea how long she'd been standing there when she felt an arm around her waist, and she looked down to see Macy standing beside her wearing a wicked grin.

"I was doing the exact same thing a few minutes before you pulled up." Macy trailed her hand down Beck's arm and threaded her fingers through hers. "Shall we go upstairs?"

Beck's entire body screamed yes, but her brain said she needed to get work out of the way first or she wouldn't be able to relax. She bent down and kissed Macy. A soft, gentle kiss she hoped conveyed the promise of more. "Yes. In a little bit. Do you mind if I show you something first? In the war room?"

Macy patted her chest. "A woman after my own heart. Like I'm ever going to say no to a little game of solving a mystery foreplay."

"You're hilarious." She held up her phone. "Come on. It's important."

Once they were in the room, Beck walked her through everything she'd learned about the two new cases.

"So, the big difference is the killer is more disorganized," Macy said.

"True, but that's a clue in itself." Beck paused for a moment to gather her thoughts. "He's more disorganized for a reason."

"He could be decompensating. Some serial killers start to really lose it and it affects their ability to control their behavior."

"Or he's not in great shape anymore." Beck started to warm up to the idea. "If this is the Parks and Rec Killer, he's ten years older than he was at the time of the original killings. Everything about these murders is the same as the ones from ten years ago, except the signs of a scuffle at the place where the body was found. He's still able to lure them off the path, but when he tries to subdue them, he's not as strong or quick or agile as he was before. He could have an injury or maybe it's a factor of his age."

Macy pinned notes on the wall while they talked, and when they were done hashing out all the facts she'd recorded from the new case, they both stood back to appraise her work.

"I feel like we're closer," Beck said.

Macy reached over and clasped her hand. "Me too."

Her touch was simple, yet electric, and Beck's body began to hum with anticipation. "Best foreplay ever."

"Does that mean I can take you upstairs now?"

"Please."

Macy turned her engine back on to get the AC blowing. She'd been waiting in the parking lot of the White Rock substation for the last hour and, despite the early hour, the heat was already stifling. Her plan had been to waylay Claire Hanlon the minute she showed up, but either Claire had snuck in a back way, or she was sleeping in this Friday morning.

Her mind flashed to the image of Beck, snuggled up next to her in bed this morning. She'd wanted to crawl under the covers and stay there with her the rest of the day, but Beck had to be at work early, so she'd decided this was the perfect opportunity to try to catch Claire Hanlon, not at a crime scene. Tomorrow though. She had big plans for spending tomorrow morning in bed with Beck.

While she waited, she signed in to Unfrozen on her phone, and while she waited for the app to load, she replayed everything she'd learned from Beck last night. If the Parks and Rec Killer was back, he wasn't as capable as he used to be at subduing his victims. Most people would wonder why he didn't use a weapon to compensate, but she knew that if it was the same guy, he would want to duplicate the experience of the first set of kills as much as possible, especially since these new murders were to celebrate a very special anniversary. She typed all of the information she'd learned into the thread she'd started the other day and made a note to check out Bruce Kehler's age. If Huntsman363 was online, he'd probably have Kehler's entire bio by the time she finished here.

When she looked up from her phone, she spotted Claire Hanlon getting out of her car a few feet away. She climbed out of her car and walked briskly toward her. "Detective Hanlon," she called out to keep Claire from trying to pretend she didn't see her.

"No press today. We'll have a briefing in the morning from HQ. You can go there now if you want to get a good seat."

Claire's eyes were red, and she looked like she hadn't slept in a week. Macy could imagine all the flack she was taking from the parents of the dead girls, her boss, and the mayor's office, on top of having to run the investigation herself. She wanted to let her off easy, but she wanted information more.

"I don't think you want me asking the questions I plan to ask in front of all the cameras tomorrow. How about you invite me in, and, in the privacy of your office, I'll give you a preview of what I plan to write, and you can decide if you want to comment?"

Claire stared at her for a moment as if her piercing gaze was a truth ray. After what seemed like forever, she sighed. "Come on."

Macy followed her into the building and to Claire's office. Claire settled into the big leather chair behind her desk and motioned for Macy to sit across from her. She ignored the invitation and walked the perimeter of the room, noting the many framed photographs.

"Did you come here to sightsee or talk to me?"

Macy finished her round of her room and took her seat. "I don't see any photos of you and Bruce Kehler. Rumor is you two were close. Wasn't he a friend of your father's?"

"They served together. A long time ago. Not that that's any of your business. Come on, Moran, why are you really here?"

"I have reason to believe the killer you're investigating now is the Parks and Rec Killer." She let the words sit for a moment to be sure she had Claire's attention before she dropped the next bomb. "And I think it might be a cop."

Claire's eyes narrowed and she slapped a hand on her desk. "That's it? That's the bomb you plan to drop at the press conference tomorrow?"

"It's not a bomb if there's no truth to it."

"You know that's not true. You go around spreading rumors like this and you'll start a panic. People will start mistrusting law enforcement at the very time they need them."

"Maybe that's not a bad thing."

"Remember that when you need one of us to respond to a call, but the bad guys aren't threatened when we get there."

"Come on, Claire," Macy said, hoping she could appeal to her, human to human. "Look at the facts. The means and mode of death are exactly the same in each case, past and present. The crime scenes are unusually devoid of forensic evidence. Someone knew exactly what they were doing. They were able to easily lure their victims off the trail. That points to two kinds of perpetrators— ones that knew the victims and ones that the victim would trust as a matter of course. You know there's not enough of a connection between all of the victims for it to be someone they all knew, but wouldn't they be likely to trust a cop?"

"I suppose you even have a theory about who it might be?"

Macy was a little surprised Claire hadn't led with an outright denial. Should she trust her gut and tell Claire who she suspected? "I'm not sure you'd believe me if I told you."

Claire leaned back in her chair and crossed her arms. "Try me."

"Fine." Macy chose her next words carefully. "I said the crime scenes were devoid of forensic evidence, which is almost true. I know you got enough DNA from the last scene to match it with a suspect. And the scenes were messier. Like he had to fight to subdue the victims."

"Which probably means the present-day killer is not the Parks and Rec Killer."

"Or it's the same person and he's rusty at it. Or not as nimble as he was ten years ago. Whoever it was had no trouble getting his victims off the beaten path. Do you think Bruce Kehler still fits in his uniform?"

Claire's face flushed a deep red. "We're done here."

"Come on, Claire. He 'investigated' the original cases," Macy said, using air quotes to emphasize investigated. "He was uniquely positioned to commit these crimes and make sure to leave no evidence behind. Hell, he left the Parks and Rec Killer files behind as cold cases, but he didn't even leave any indication they were connected. He was forced to retire over how he handled Frank Flynn's case. Do you honestly think that a guy who would withhold evidence in a murder case and stand by to watch an innocent man go to prison for life wouldn't also be capable of committing murder himself? He's older now, so he's not as good at it as he was before, but I think he's still doing it."

Claire stood. "I'll tell you what I think. I think you've lost your freaking mind. I don't know how you know what you do about these cases, but there's a big difference between taking misguided actions to deliver what you believe to be justice and going on a brutal killing spree." She pointed to the door. "Go."

Macy wanted to protest, to try to continue the conversation, but she could tell by the angry look on Claire's face, she'd reached her limit today. Outside in her car, she sat in the quiet for a few minutes, wondering why she'd let the conversation get so completely out of hand. When she'd arrived, she'd planned to float her theory in vague terms to see if Claire would bite, but instead she'd fired a shotgun in the water and killed any chance Claire would ever speak to her about these cases again.

She replayed everything she'd said. She'd believed every word, but as she reeled them back in she realized she'd overplayed her hand by giving away the fact she knew things she shouldn't. Things Beck had told her in confidence. Things that could get Beck in deep shit. Sending the info in to Unfrozen under her anonymous handle was one thing, but she'd spouted off to one of Beck's fellow officers. She picked up her phone and fired off a text. *Any chance you can get away for lunch?*

She watched the screen for a few minutes. No little bubbles indicating Beck was typing a response. Nothing. She started to send a second text and decided she would only make things worse if she looked like she was in a panic. She took a few deep breaths. Claire wasn't going to connect what she'd told her with Beck. She doubted Beck had told anyone they were an item, and she hadn't told anyone but Wayne. She was overthinking things. She'd see Beck again tonight as planned and everything would be fine.

She really, really needed it to be.

CHAPTER TWENTY-ONE

Beck stared at the text on her phone and blinked. *Get in here now.* She didn't recognize the number, but she only knew one person who summoned her so abruptly on a regular basis, though she usually did so via the office intercom. She stood and walked to Mendoza's door.

"Come in." Mendoza barked the words, and her tone was as gruff as the expression on her face. It had already been a long day. Councilwoman Villa had been here for much of it, pulling random files and asking her questions. She didn't mind the work—it had been nice to have someone in the file room to interact with, someone who seemed to care about these forgotten cases—but she'd had to miss the opportunity to have lunch with Macy because of it. *You'll see her in a few hours.* She smiled at the thought.

"Sit down and stop smiling. I need to ask you some questions."

Beck sat but stayed on the edge of the seat, sensing she needed to be on guard.

"When did you decide it was okay to feed information to a reporter?"

It took every ounce of self-control she had not to react to the question, but on the inside she started to panic, wondering what Mendoza knew and how she knew it. She could play this two ways. She could lie and say she didn't know what Mendoza was talking about or she could confess she'd shared information about the pending investigations and cold cases with Macy. While she sorted out which path she should take, she came up with a third approach. Stall. "Are you talking about the interview I gave to the *Dallas Gazette*? Because, other than personal background information that is mine to share, I didn't say anything to them that I didn't say in open court."

Mendoza scowled. "You know that's not what I'm talking about." She placed both hands on the desk and leaned forward. "Let me tell you what I think happened. You've been spending all this time with Villa and she's gotten in your head, so you decide you're going to play detective and start trying to solve some of these old cases on your own. Which I've already told you is pointless. But you're not content to settle for digging up ancient crimes. No, you're a real big shot, so you start looking at current cases and feeding information to Macy Moran whose only mission is to embarrass this department. Tell me I'm wrong."

She wasn't wrong. She wasn't entirely right either, but Mendoza's growl said she wasn't interested in parsing the details. But Beck did have questions, and if she was in trouble anyway, she may as well risk more of Mendoza's wrath by asking them. "What makes you think Macy Moran wants to embarrass the department?"

"Because that's exactly what she's doing. She showed up at Claire Hanlon's office this morning spouting some crap about all of these cases, past and present, being the work of a cop. She even named names."

She kept talking, but her voice was a dull buzz against the noise in Beck's head. Macy had used the information she'd given her, not to investigate on her own, but to try to shame the department? *She even named names.* Who did she accuse? And if she thought she knew who committed these crimes, why hadn't she shared that information with her? After all she'd done to help, at great risk to herself, she expected more. Had Macy been playing her all along?

"...suspended. Effective immediately."

She tuned back in as Mendoza dropped the proclamation like a hammer, and it took her a second to comprehend what was happening. "What?"

"Give me your shield and your service weapon and get the fuck out." Mendoza smirked. "Have fun explaining to ADA Neely why his star witness has a big fat blemish on her record."

She was reeling from the attack as she left Mendoza's office. Foster wasn't at his desk, and she wondered if he'd been released back to active duty. At least she wouldn't have to work with Mendoza without him as a buffer. But her relief was short-lived when she realized she wouldn't be working at all for the foreseeable future. And Jack's case. Had she just tanked it by putting her own credibility into question?

Within minutes, she was in her Jeep on the road, barely conscious of her destination until she pulled into Macy's driveway. She didn't have any recollection about making the choice to come here, but she knew it was where she needed to be. She couldn't fix anything else about her crumbling life until she confronted Macy and found out if she had done what Mendoza said. Macy's car was nowhere in sight, so she didn't bother ringing the bell. Instead, she sat in the front porch swing and waited, praying this was all a big misunderstanding.

❖

Macy spotted Beck's Jeep in her driveway from down the street, and for a brief second, she contemplated turning around and driving in the opposite direction.

Maybe she doesn't know.

But Macy knew in her gut that Beck already knew, and if she didn't face her now, they would never get past it. They might never get past it anyway, but Beck was the kind of woman worth fighting for. She hoped Beck thought the same about her.

She parked her car next to Beck's and walked to the front door. Beck was sitting in the porch swing, leaning back with her eyes shut. Macy walked softly toward her, not wanting to wake her if she was indeed sleeping, and she nearly jumped out of her skin when Beck spoke.

"Surprised to see me here?"

There was an edge to Beck's tone she'd never heard before. It was sharper than when she'd first confronted Beck outside of Jack Staples's hearing and she knew this time it was a deeper cut because it was directed at her personally instead of at her profession. "Pleasantly surprised, yes. I mean, I was hoping to see you later tonight, but earlier is better."

"Not when earlier means I've been fired."

Macy sank into onto the bench across from the swing. "Oh no, Beck."

"Suspended, indefinitely. And I think you know why."

"I really don't." She didn't mean to sound disingenuous, but it wasn't possible Claire had connected the dots and pegged Beck for the leak so quickly. Was it?

"You went to see Claire Hanlon this morning."

It wasn't a question, but she knew Beck expected an answer. "True."

"And you told her you believe the Parks and Rec Killer and whoever killed Jody Nelson and Marisol Garza is a cop."

"I did."

"Who?"

Macy was confused for a second until she realized Beck was asking for the name. She owed her that much. "I think it was Bruce Kehler, the lead detective on the Parks and Rec cases."

"Based on information I shared with you."

"Yes."

"Yet, you didn't feel compelled to share your theory with me?"

Not the angle she'd been expecting, and Macy felt anger of her own start to bubble to the surface in the face of Beck's indignation. "Is that why you're angry? That I didn't tell you my theory? What would you have said exactly if I'd told you who I thought the killer was, make that *is* a cop, let alone that it was one who'd conducted the investigation?"

She watched the struggle play out on Beck's face, but she wasn't inclined to help her along. Maybe the consequences of turning in her partner had caused Beck to swing 180 degrees in the other direction, and she was no longer willing to accept her brothers and sisters in blue could do any wrong. But the woman she'd come to know wasn't like that. She'd risked giving her information without any qualification about where it led, but she'd had a right to expect Macy wouldn't share what she'd told her without the courtesy of checking with her first. It was a matter of respect, and she was in the wrong. Admitting it was the only way she'd have a chance at diffusing this situation.

"I was wrong to tell Hanlon the things you told me. I didn't tell her the info came from you, but I should've anticipated she would figure it out."

"I'm the one that broke the rules," Beck replied, her voice slightly softer. "I never should've…"

"Trusted me?" Macy finished her sentence and tried not to get riled. "Respectfully, you're wrong about that. Who else is going to look at things objectively? You're sitting here right now in denial that the killer could be one of your own. Claire Hanlon practically threw me out of her office when I suggested it. I'm the only one who isn't looking at these cases with an agenda other than to find the killer, whoever it is." She reached out and put her hand on Beck's knee. "I only want the truth and I want to find it with you. And I'll do whatever it takes to help you get your job back if that's what you want. You can trust me on that."

She watched Beck's expression start to soften and she prayed she hadn't completely blown it. Beck was the best thing that had happened to her in a long time, and she couldn't bear the idea she'd caused her so much pain.

"I don't know what to say."

"That's fair," Macy said. "While you think about it, why don't you come inside, and I'll order us some dinner?"

Beck nodded and Macy extended her hand and helped her to her feet. As she started to put her arm around Beck's waist, her phone buzzed in her other hand and she fumbled to silence it, dropping it on the wood planks of the porch where it skittered under the porch swing. Beck bent down to retrieve and it and started to hand it to her, but then pulled it close to her face.

Macy watched her eyes widen and a knot formed in her stomach. "What is it?"

Beck handed her the phone like it was a poisonous snake. "You tell me."

Macy took the phone from her hand and read the message on the screen. It was from Jerry, and it was short and simple. *Need your profile on Jack by noon tomorrow. Make it good.*

Damn it, Jerry. She hadn't interviewed Jack and had no intention of writing the piece, but Jerry was under pressure from Holt Baxter and his way of dealing with it was to apply his own pressure to her.

"Is that you being objective? You're going to tell Jack's side of the story and let the readers figure out the truth?"

She looked up into Beck's eyes and was struck by the disappointment she saw reflected there, and she was desperate to make it disappear. "Beck, you have to believe me—"

Beck held up her palm. "Just stop." She waved a hand between them. "This was a mistake, and it's over."

She turned and walked away. Macy scrambled to say something to get Beck to turn around and change her mind, but for the first time in her life, she couldn't find the right words. She was sorry she'd hurt Beck, but she stood by her quest to find the truth. In the face of what she viewed as betrayal, Beck would never believe she hadn't planned to tell Jack's side, and if Beck didn't trust her, they'd probably never make it anyway. She'd been alone most of her life. Why should things be any different now?

Because going back to her solitary life now was worse than if she'd never had a taste of what it would be like to be with a woman who understood her. If only she hadn't been wrong.

CHAPTER TWENTY-TWO

Beck woke to the unpleasant glare of bright light shining through her eyelids and pulled the sheet up over her head. "Please, God, turn it off," she mumbled.

"I would, but alas, I have no control over the sun."

She lowered the sheet and opened her eyes to find Liam towering over her. "Sit down, you're hurting my neck."

He rolled his eyes but sat at the end of her bed. "I made dinner."

"Dinner?"

"It's a meal. People eat it in the evening. What part of this conversation is unclear?"

She shot up in bed. "What time is it?"

"It's six. I know it's early for dinner, but one of our clients brought over some new salads they are trying out at their restaurant for lunch, and I ate one to be nice, and it was great, but an hour later I was starving and I haven't had a chance to eat, so I figured we could eat early and maybe watch a movie. Or talk. Talking would be good."

When had Liam become such a Chatty Cathy? Beck rubbed her eyes and willed him to stop talking. "I know you just said a bunch of things, but all I heard was the time." She swung her legs out of the bed. "I need to get in a run." She stood and started searching for her shoes.

"I really was hoping we could talk. You've been back here a week and you're welcome to stay as long as you want, but I'm a little worried about you. All you do is run and sleep, run and sleep."

She paused midway in her search and looked at him. She could tell he was genuinely concerned, but she didn't want to talk about anything that had to do with her job or Macy, and anything else was fluff. If she told him what she was up to, he'd do everything he could to stop her, so it was easier not to share at all even though she could tell it pained him to see her pulling inward. "I should go back to my place."

Liam shook his head. "No, you shouldn't, and I'm not asking you too." He smiled. "I like having you here. I can't help it that I want to fix things, but I can't help if I don't know what's wrong."

She sighed and sat back down beside him. "I got suspended."

"That much I figured out."

"For helping Macy."

"Helping her rob a bank? Commit a burglary?"

"Very funny." She reached for the right words to convey exactly what happened without casting judgment because even though she knew Liam would take her side no matter what, some part of her didn't want Liam to dislike Macy. She couldn't explain it, and she knew it wasn't rational, but that's how it was. "I leaked information to help her with an investigation. She wasn't very discreet about it and it got back to my boss. Hence the suspension."

"And you cut things off with her because of that?" His tone was very matter-of-fact.

"How do you know I cut things off with her?"

"Because you're not the only one with keen powers of observation. I've seen you ignoring texts and calls. You've been here for a week, and, except for your incessant running habit, you don't go anywhere else. It's pretty clear you're in classic avoidance mode."

"It's whatever. Macy and I aren't a thing."

"Too bad. I like her."

She wanted to say she thought it was too bad too, but if she started down that path, she'd wind up feeling conflicted again, and she was just starting to be okay with ambivalence when it came to Macy Moran. At least she pretended to be okay, and that was all she could do until the real thing kicked in.

She spotted her shoes under the nightstand and reached for them. "Everything's going to be fine."

"But you're going for a run instead of eating dinner?"

"I'll eat something when I get back. I promise." She stood and walked to the door. Before she left, she turned back to see him still sitting on her bed, or rather his guest room bed. "I appreciate you letting me crash with you. I promise I'm not running away from anything. I just need some time to work things out."

"I love you."

"I love you too." She could feel tears start to well up and she turned and brushed her hand across her face. "See you later," she called out and then took off before things got even more mushy.

She retrieved her Jeep from behind the building and while it warmed up, she retrieved a map of White Rock Lake from her pocket. She'd marked in red all the trails she'd run over the past week, but there were still three she hadn't tried. She'd run one tonight and one in the morning and the last one tomorrow night, and then she'd start all over again. It wasn't a great or foolproof plan, but if the killer was out there, then eventually she'd come across him. It was just a matter of statistics, and now that she didn't have a job to go to, she had all the time she needed to get the numbers to work in her favor. She'd lost a lot over the past few months. Her police family, Macy, her job. She might not be able to do anything about the first two, but earning back her badge would be a start toward building back her life and she was determined to show everyone why she'd earned it in the first place.

Chapter Twenty-three

Macy squinted at her computer and tried to figure out exactly what she was looking at. After days of sitting in her study, staring at the wall, at her notes, at her computer screen, her eyes were blurry and her brain was on overload, and she no longer trusted her ability to tell fact from fiction.

She typed her question into the message box: *What is this?*

Within seconds, Huntsman363 responded: *That's Bruce Kehler's signature. Want to know where I found it?*

She did and she didn't. Every time Bruce's name came up, it was a painful reminder of Beck walking away from her and never looking back. It had been a week since they'd parted ways on her front porch. She'd reached out a couple of times to check in, but Beck hadn't returned any of her texts. She'd even gone next level amateur detective aka stalker, and gone by Beck's apartment, but her Jeep hadn't been there, even late at night. Could she have moved on already?

No, Beck didn't seem like the kind of person who got involved lightly, and she'd probably take some time for herself before moving on. Would that time give her a different perspective?

Macy wondered when she'd become such an optimist, holding out hope she and Beck could reconnect, put their differences behind them, and find a way forward. Other women had come and gone, and she'd forgotten them quickly, but Beck had been different.

She turned her focus back to the computer, reread Huntsman363's question, and typed, *Sure.*

A larger photo appeared in the thread. It was a lined page with a bunch of signatures, including the one he'd just shown her. She scanned the entire page and froze when she reached a typed line at the bottom. *Vincent and Sons Funeral Home, Madison, NJ.* She traced her finger along the photo, reading the other names on the page. Bruce's was the only one she recognized, but there was something about the context she couldn't shake. She pulled her laptop toward her and typed the name of the funeral home in the search bar and while it churned out results, she turned back to her conversation with Huntsman363, who she was now beginning to view with suspicion.

My curiosity is definitely piqued. Tell me more?

She hit send and turned back to the laptop, selecting the link for the funeral home's website. A few clicks later, she found their virtual guestbook, and she stared at it for a moment before typing in a name.

Do you really want me to tell you everything? Isn't it more fun to find these things out on your own?

She glanced at the message out of the corner of her eye while still watching the funeral home website which was agonizingly slow. Huntsman363 was taunting her. But why? Sure, sometimes wackos made it onto Unfrozen, but they usually showed their crazy within a few posts and were banned from the site. He'd been fairly neutral on all of their interactions up until now, but something had changed.

She started to type a reply to him, but the funeral home page stopped loading at that point and the results of her search appeared on the screen. *Cathy Paxton, 71, survived by her husband, Wayne Paxton.* There was more—the usual stuff contained in most obituaries. She skipped it and scrolled down to the guestbook for Cathy. The virtual signatures and sympathy notes were all in the same perfect cursive, but a few pages in, she started seeing what looked like scanned pages of the in-person guestbook. She kept clicking until she landed on a photo that was an exact copy of the one Huntsman363 had sent. Bruce Kehler's name was the third one from the top.

What did it mean? Had Bruce Kehler attended the funeral for Wayne's wife, and if so, why? Her brain started firing in a dozen different directions, starting with why Huntsman363 had sent her this information in the first place.

Normally, I would rather do my own research, but I might be out of my depth here. Help a girl out?

She waited, hoping her appeal to his ego would buy her some insight. She didn't have to wait long.

Don't be shy, Macy. I know you know who I am. Beck gave you everything you need to know. How is she by the way?

She shoved her chair back and stood, whipping her head around the room as if she could spot someone watching her. But the blinds were shut, and the door was locked and she was completely alone. She walked the room anyway, looking for any sign she was being surveilled. Satisfied she was secure, she returned to her computer and read the message again. *I know you know who I am. Beck gave you everything you need.*

Bruce had been at Wayne's wife's funeral. Had they been friends? Had Bruce cozied up to Wayne because he was the reporter covering the Parks and Rec Killer? It would be exactly the kind of sick and twisted thing a serial killer would do.

How is she by the way?

Macy's heart raced and she went cold. Was Beck in danger?

If Beck was in danger, it was because of her. Because of the fact she'd told Claire Hanlon she thought Bruce was the killer and Claire had incorrectly assumed Beck had led her to that conclusion. She needed to set the record straight. She should call Claire. Wait, what good would that do? Claire wasn't about to believe anything she said. Claire was a good cop, but Bruce had been her mentor, and for all she knew, Claire still harbored loyalty toward him. She may have even told Bruce everything she'd said about him. No, what she needed to do was get in touch with Beck. Beck who was never home and wouldn't return her calls.

She looked at the clock. It was five a.m. Surely, Beck would be home at this time of the morning. She looked at her computer and contemplated whether she should respond to Huntsman363's last message, before deciding against it. Let him wonder where she'd gone.

She made it to Beck's apartment in record time. She didn't spot her Jeep in the parking lot, but she decided to go ahead and knock on her door. She knocked lightly at first, stopping to text her, before she resumed, this time much harder.

"What's going on?"

She looked up to see one of Beck's neighbors poking his head out his door. "Sorry. I'm looking for your neighbor. Do you know her?"

"Sure, but she's not here. She hasn't been here all week."

Macy glanced at her phone, but Beck hadn't responded to her 911 text. "Do you happen to know where she's staying? I'm a friend." She smiled to make her seem like the kind of person someone would want to be friends with instead of an insane person who tried to beat down people's doors at o'dark thirty.

"Don't have a clue. Sorry."

The guy shut the door quickly as if afraid she'd ask more questions. She looked at her phone again and resent the text to Beck with a few extra exclamation points, while she decided what to do next. It was dark and Beck could be anywhere. She hadn't been here all week. Maybe she'd gone out of town? Which would be good right? Because if she was out of town, she was out of danger. But she needed to know for sure.

Liam. Beck's brother's name popped in her head, and she immediately started googling him. She didn't find a residential listing—not like anyone had a home landline anymore—but she did find a business listing for Ramsey Advertising in Deep Ellum. Logic told her they wouldn't be open at five thirty in the morning, but she plugged the address in her phone and dialed the number the second she got back in her car.

"Thank you for contacting Ramsey Advertising. Our regular business hours are…"

She almost hung up, but decided it was better to cover her bases, and when the voice mail beeped, she left what she hoped was a non-crazy, but urgent sounding message asking Liam to contact her right away. She was two blocks from his office when her phone rang.

"Moran, here."

"Macy?"

She'd prayed it would be Beck on the other line, but the deep male voice was the next best thing. "Liam? Do you know where Beck is? I was just at her apartment and her neighbors said she hasn't been home in a week. I'm outside your office because I didn't know where else to go."

"Hang on, let me check."

She parked in front of his building while she was on hold and waited, impatiently, for him to return to the phone. A few minutes later, the front door to the building opened and Liam walked out and over to the passenger side of her car and knocked on the window. She unlocked the door and he climbed inside.

"She's been staying with me." He pointed to the top of the building. "I have a loft above the biz. But she's not here."

Her mind started racing. "Do you know where she is?"

"Out for a run. She's been kind of obsessed with running since you two broke things off. She gets in at least two a day, morning and night. I'm beginning to think she's secretly training for a marathon."

Macy recalled Beck mentioning she liked to run, but she'd specifically mentioned mornings and the paths at the Village Country Club where her apartment was located. Surely she wouldn't drive all the way back there to get in her morning run if she was staying with Liam. "Do you know where she runs?"

She could hear the tremor in her voice and apparently Liam could too.

"Macy, what's going on?"

"I think she might be in trouble. Do you know where she is?"

"Hang on."

Macy watched him run back inside the building wishing she knew what the hell he was doing. She looked at her phone again, praying for a text from Beck, but all that was there were her urgent messages, begging Beck to return her call. Either she was really in trouble or she really, really didn't want to talk to her.

Liam burst out of the building and jumped back into her car. He shoved a piece of paper at her. "I found this in her room. I've seen her writing on it whenever she comes back from a run. I figured it was like a training log, but it's a map. Look." He pointed at the red Xs scattered around the body of water. "Do you make anything of it?"

She stared at the map of White Rock Lake and suddenly she knew exactly why Beck was running night and day. "Yes. Buckle up." She slammed on the accelerator and took the first turn, hoping they weren't too late.

Beck placed her foot on the stone bench and extended her leg to stretch. All the running she'd done over the course of the past week had started to take its toll on her muscles. If today was a bust, she was going to have to take off tomorrow to rest and revisit her strategy.

She'd been certain whoever the Parks and Rec Killer was, he would strike again at White Rock Lake. It had been his most popular spot ten years ago, and the recent killings had both occurred nearby. She'd finished her first round through the list of ideal locations to lure someone off the trail and commit a murder undetected last night, so this morning she was back to spot number one. The place where Jody Nelson's body had been found. The place where she met Macy for the very first time.

As she slipped into the rhythm of her run, she allowed herself a moment to think about Macy and wonder what she was doing right now. She could almost picture her standing in the middle of her war room plotting her next move to catch the killer. Beck admired her tenacity, but she wished she wasn't so myopic. It wasn't like she wasn't open to the idea the killer might be a cop, but Macy had been absolutely convinced it was true.

What if she's right?

It wasn't the first time the thought had occurred to her since she'd last seen Macy. Bruce Kehler had resigned under a cloud of suspicion about his role in the wrongful conviction of Frank Flynn. The case had gotten a lot of press coverage at the time, but then it had faded away as if nothing ever happened. Had there been a cover-up? Had the department handled Bruce by sending him into early retirement instead of dealing with the issue head-on? Would they have done something similar with Jack if she hadn't gone public?

If that was the way they handled things, did she even want her shield back?

Yes, she did. Her mom had believed police work was a calling, and she was certain her mom had been right. What kind of person would she be if she ditched it all simply because the profession attracted some bad seeds? Besides, she honestly thought Macy was wrong about Bruce being the killer. He might have had the opportunity, but he'd been a decorated cop who'd risen through the ranks. Yes, he'd made mistakes, costly ones, when he'd been a detective, but he wasn't stupid, and he could've done more to throw suspicion off himself if he was the Parks and Rec Killer. Macy had the right idea about the killer resurfacing in a macabre celebration of the ten-year anniversary, but she wasn't convinced she had the right suspect.

As she approached the area of the trail near where Jody's body had been found, she slowed to a walk, lifting first one foot and then the other behind her to stretch her calves. She'd just finished her stretch when she heard a voice from behind her.

"Excuse me."

She turned slowly, allowing her gaze to sweep the perimeter as she looked for the man speaking. It was still dark outside, and the nearest lamppost was about thirty feet away. She could make out a shape coming toward her, about her height, stocky. As he came closer, she noted he was wearing jeans, black tennis shoes, and a plain black T-shirt. He didn't look like a runner, but he could be on an innocent morning walk. Or something else, not so innocent.

She crossed her arms in front of her chest, letting one hand rest on the butt of her gun in the shoulder holster she wore under her jacket. She was already sweating from the run and the bulk of the jacket, which was way too hot for a June morning, but it was the only way she could conceal her weapon. He looked harmless, but she wasn't ready to make a final assessment.

"Do you happen to know if this trail leads to the dog park?"

He kept walking as he talked, and he was only a few steps away from her when he finished his seemingly innocuous question. Except he didn't have a dog with him, or even a leash for a prop, and she was certain she recognized his face, but before she could place it, she heard another voice and this one was calling her name.

She squinted to try to see who was running toward them and was shocked when Macy burst into sight. Macy stopped short next to the man and addressed him first. "Wayne?" she said, seemingly startled by his presence.

Beck saw a flash of anger cross his face which he quickly covered with a smile, and she remembered where she'd seen him. He was the reporter who'd written all the articles about the Parks and Rec Killer. Wayne Paxton. She'd seen his face on a feature piece he did about the serial killer. He'd covered every detail of each of the murders in excruciating detail, and cold certainty swept through her. There was a reason he knew every detail, and it wasn't because he was a great reporter.

"Macy," she said. "Can I talk to you?"

Macy looked from Wayne to her and back again. "What are you both doing here together?"

Beck willed Macy to read her mind. "Just a quick minute." She jerked her chin to the right, desperate to get Macy to step away from Wayne. "Alone."

Macy continued to look at her with a puzzled expression. She was going to have to find another way to intervene. She considered her options and decided pulling out her gun right now, with Macy this close to Wayne could turn into a disaster, so she settled on surprise as her best weapon, and she prepared to run toward Wayne and knock him to the ground.

She was two steps in when he pulled out a knife. She'd barely made it a third step when he grabbed Macy with one hand and held the knife to her neck with the other. Her heart wrenched as she watched Macy's face morph from surprise to dread, and she reached for her gun.

"Drop it or I'll slit her throat."

Beck lowered her gun but didn't let go. "I have a feeling you're going to do that anyway."

His laugh was hollow. "I might. I never had to before, but then again I had much more cooperative subjects." He looked down at Macy. "You always were a fighter, but look at you being quiet when it counts."

"Don't listen to him, Macy. I've got you."

"On the contrary," he said. "I've got her. Now put the gun down."

He growled the last words. Beck stared at Macy willing her to stay calm while she thought of a way out. She was staring so intently, she almost missed seeing a tall shadow approaching from behind them. Not wanting Wayne to notice whoever it was, she started lowering her gun hand to the ground to keep him focused on her. She had just released the weapon when Liam's face came into sight a few feet behind Wayne and Macy. This was her best chance, and she took it.

She pointed over Wayne's right shoulder and shouted, "He's got a knife." She was running toward them before she finished her yell. Wayne hadn't been tricked into turning his head, but Liam grabbed his arm from behind and held it far enough away from Macy's neck that Beck was able to snatch her completely out of his grasp and they both fell to the ground.

"Stay down," she said and sprang to her feet to join Liam, who now had Wayne in a head lock.

"I've got him," Liam said.

Beck pulled out her phone and dialed 911, giving them the nearest trail marker. She picked up her gun and joined Macy on the ground while she kept the barrel trained on Wayne.

"Are you okay?"

"It was Wayne. How could it be Wayne? How could I have been so wrong?"

Macy's voice was hazy, and her eyes were dark. Beck held her close. "It doesn't matter. You're okay. Nothing else matters."

"He was going to kill me."

Beck shook her head. "I would never have let that happen." She kissed Macy's head. "You and me? We're not done yet."

Macy clutched her arm. "He could've killed you too." She shuddered. "I don't know what I'd do if something happened to you."

Beck pulled her closer. "Nothing's going to happen to either of us. Nothing we can't handle, anyway."

In a few minutes, the sun would come up and the park would be swarming with cops. They would pull her aside and take her in for questioning. She was prepared for the scrutiny, for the questions, for whatever came next, but when it was done, she was going to find Macy and together they would find a way to put all of this behind them and start over.

CHAPTER TWENTY-FOUR

Macy barely recognized her own house. There were fresh flowers in every room on the first floor, music floating through the air, and a banner hanging from the balcony that screamed *Congratulations* with a bunch of extra exclamation points.

"You think it's too much, don't you?"

She'd been so focused on the contents of her study for the past ten years, she hadn't given much thought to sprucing up the rest of the house, but Harrison had worked wonders. She gave him a big smile. "Not at all. I think it's perfect."

Donna walked out of the kitchen and rubbed her hands together. "The cake came out perfectly. I hope you were serious when you said she likes chocolate because it's chocolate to the tenth power covered in more chocolate and wrapped in a cloud of chocolate."

"I'm sure she'll love it."

The doorbell rang and they all turned toward it at the same time. "Are you going to get it?" Harrison asked.

"You do it," Macy said. "I want to watch her face when she comes in the door."

Harrison ran to the door and flung it open. Beck was standing on the porch next to Liam. She hesitated for a moment, staring at the banner that was right in her sightline. She smiled and then scanned the room. Macy stood perfectly still, anxiously waiting for the moment Beck's eyes met hers. They'd spent most of their time together in the month since Wayne was arrested, but today was different. Today, Beck had been officially reinstated as a Dallas police detective, and as if on cue, she reached into her pocket, pulled out her shield, and held it high while the rest of them clapped and shouted congratulations.

Donna hustled them all into the dining room where she handed out glasses of Champagne. She pointed to the very large cake in the center of the table. "I'm serving," she said, brandishing a spatula. "Prepare to enter food coma status."

They all sat around the table while Donna handed out gigantic slices. Once everyone had a piece of cake, Macy clanged her fork against her glass and called for attention. "Congratulations to Detective Beck Ramsey, the newest member of the crimes against persons unit at the White Rock substation."

Beck half stood and bowed to the applause. "Thank you, everyone. Claire Hanlon asked for me to be assigned to her unit, and since she's on the fast track to become a chief, I'm flattered. And I have a feeling I know who put a bug in her ear."

Macy smiled when Beck shot a look at her. "I may have showed up at her office and made it clear I was very wrong about this case, that your instincts were spot-on, and that you were exactly the kind of cop she needs on her team. The kind who isn't afraid to speak truth to power but is also committed to law enforcement as a noble cause."

"Apparently, she bought it." Beck tipped her glass in Macy's direction. "And congratulations to this one. Part one of her feature piece on the Parks and Rec Killer runs this weekend."

"I have to say, I've never been so excited to be done with a story."

"I'm sure the folks at the Baxter Group will be thrilled with the bump in advertising dollars they get from it," Liam said. He flinched. "I'm sorry, that was really insensitive. I know the guy was your friend. This had to be a really difficult piece to write."

"Less than you'd think. I've spent the last month thinking about Wayne, and all I feel is anger. He murdered my best friend, and he would've killed Beck and me too if he could. When it comes to him, it's not like I'm mourning the loss of someone I cared about. He was never the person I thought he was. If his wife hadn't fallen ill, there's no telling how many other women he'd have killed, and I'm happy to know he'll rot in prison for the rest of his miserable life." She laughed. "Don't get me wrong, I'm sure there's therapy ahead, but I can finally turn my study into something other than a war room."

"And as for the Baxter Group, they can kiss my ass. I handed in the story and gave my notice. The social media group Leaderboard wants to expand into online news platforms and you're looking at their new feature editor. I start in two weeks."

The group applauded again. Harrison raised his fork in the air. "I'm really happy for you all and your great news, but if we don't get to eat this cake soon, I'm going to waste away."

Beck stood. "Sorry, Harrison, but I have one more piece of news. Jack Staples signed off on a plea agreement this morning. They still have to have a presentence report done before they determine the final sentence, but I won't have to testify." She waved her arm. "Let the cake eating commence."

Later, after everyone had left, Macy was putting dishes in the dishwasher when Beck slipped up behind her and pulled her into a hug. Macy turned into her arms. "I could get used to this."

"Me too." She cocked her head. "Are you really okay? You've been through a lot lately. I know you joked about Wayne earlier, but being betrayed like that had to hurt more than you've let on."

Macy sighed. "It did. Finishing this piece is giving me some closure. I guess if time doesn't heal all wounds, then I'll get some help." She ran her hand along Beck's arm. "What about you? After all you've gone through after turning Jack in, are you more relieved or angry that he's pleading guilty?"

Beck didn't hesitate. "It's a relief. Do I think everyone is going to instantly like me again? Probably not, but I have the approval of the only people I care about—you and Liam."

"Our lives have changed a lot since we met."

"Truth."

"Do you think you might be ready for one more change?" Macy took a deep breath. "Because this is a really big house and now that I'm going to be spending time in other rooms besides the study, I was thinking it would be nice to share it with you." She held her breath while she waited for Beck's response.

"Nice? I'm thinking it would be more along the lines of amazing." Beck pulled her close. "Let's be amazing together."

"I think that's the perfect plan," Macy said, kissing Beck to seal the deal.

The End

About the Author

Carsen Taite's goal as an author is to spin tales with plot lines as interesting as the cases she encountered in her career as a criminal defense lawyer. She is the award-winning author of over two dozen novels of romance and romantic intrigue, including the Luca Bennett Bounty Hunter series, the Lone Star Law series, the Legal Affairs romances, and the Courting Danger series.

Books Available from Bold Strokes Books

Boy at the Window by Lauren Melissa Ellzey. Daniel Kim struggles to hold onto reality while haunted by both his very-present past and his never-present parents. Jiwon Yoon may be the only one who can break Daniel free. (978-1-63679-092-3)

Deadly Secrets by VK Powell. Corporate criminals want whistleblower Jana Elliott permanently silenced, but Rafe Silva will risk everything to keep the woman she loves safe. (978-1-63679-087-9)

Enchanted Autumn by Ursula Klein. When Elizabeth comes to Salem, Massachusetts, to study the witch trials, she never expects to find love—or an actual witch…and Hazel might just turn out to be both. (978-1-63679-104-3)

Escorted by Renee Roman. When fantasy meets reality, will escort Ryan Lewis be able to walk away from a chance at forever with her new client Dani? (978-1-63679-039-8)

Her Heart's Desire by Anne Shade. Two women. One choice. Will Eve and Lynette be able to overcome their doubts and fears to embrace their deepest desire? (978-1-63679-102-9)

My Secret Valentine by Julie Cannon, Erin Dutton, & Anne Shade. Winning the heart of your secret Valentine? These award-winning authors agree, there is no better way to fall in love. (978-1-63679-071-8)

Perilous Obsession by Carsen Taite. When reporter Macy Moran becomes consumed with solving a cold case, will her quest for the truth bring her closer to Detective Beck Ramsey or will her obsession with finding a murderer rob her of a chance at true love? (978-1-63679-009-1)

Reading Her by Amanda Radley. Lauren and Allegra learn love and happiness are right where they least expect it. There's just one problem: Lauren has a secret she cannot tell anyone, and Allegra knows she's hiding something. (978-1-63679-075-6)

The Willing by Lyn Hemphill. Kitty Wilson doesn't know how, but she can bring people back from the dead as long as someone is willing to take their place and keep the universe in balance. (978-1-63679-083-1)

Three Left Turns to Nowhere by Nathan Burgoine, J. Marshall Freeman, & Jeffrey Ricker. Three strangers heading to a convention in Toronto are stranded in rural Ontario, where a small town with a subtle kind of magic leads each to discover what he's been searching for. (978-1-63679-050-3)

Watching Over Her by Ronica Black. As they face the snowstorm of the century, and the looming threat of a stalker, Riley and Zoey just might find love in the most unexpected of places. (978-1-63679-100-5)

#shedeservedit by Greg Herren. When his gay best friend, and high school football star, is murdered, Alex Wheeler is a suspect and must find the truth to clear himself. (978-1-63555-996-5)

Always by Kris Bryant. When a pushy American private investigator shows up demanding to meet the woman in Camila's artwork, instead of introducing her to her great-grandmother, Camila decides to lead her on a wild goose chase all over Italy. (978-1-63679-027-5)

Exes and O's by Joy Argento. Ali and Madison really only have one thing in common. The girl who broke their heart may be the only one who can put it back together. (978-1-63679-017-6)

One Verse Multi by Sander Santiago. Life was good: promotion, friends, falling in love, discovering that the multi-verse is on a fast track to collision—wait, what? Good thing Martin King works for a company that can fix the problem, right…um…right? (978-1-63679-069-5)

Paris Rules by Jaime Maddox. Carly Becker has been searching for the perfect woman all her life, but no one ever seems to be just right until Paige Waterford checks all her boxes, except the most important one—she's married. (978-1-63679-077-0)

Shadow Dancers by Suzie Clarke. In this third and final book in the Moon Shadow series, Rachel must find a way to become the hunter and not the hunted, and this time she will meet Ehsee Yumiko head-on. (978-1-63555-829-6)

The Kiss by C.A. Popovich. When her wife refuses their divorce and begins to stalk her, threatening her life, Kate realizes to protect her new love, Leslie, she has to let her go, even if it breaks her heart. (978-1-63679-079-4)

The Wedding Setup by Charlotte Greene. When Ryann, a big-time New York executive, goes to Colorado to help out with her best friend's wedding, she never expects to fall for the maid of honor. (978-1-63679-033-6)

Velocity by Gun Brooke. Holly and Claire work toward an uncertain future preparing for an alien space mission, and only one thing is for certain, they will have to risk their lives, and their hearts, to discover the truth. (978-1-63555-983-5)

Wildflower Words by Sam Ledel. Lida Jones treks West with her father in search of a better life on the rapidly developing American frontier, but finds home when she meets Hazel Thompson. (978-1-63679-055-8)

A Fairer Tomorrow by Kathleen Knowles. For Maddie Weeks and Gerry Stern, the Second World War brought them together, but the end of the war might rip them apart. (978-1-63555-874-6)

Holiday Hearts by Diana Day-Admire and Lyn Cole. Opposites attract during Christmastime chaos in Kansas City. (978-1-63679-128-9)

Changing Majors by Ana Hartnett Reichardt. Beyond a love, beyond a coming-out, Bailey Sullivan discovers what lies beyond the shame and self-doubt imposed on her by traditional Southern ideals. (978-1-63679-081-7)

Fresh Grave in Grand Canyon by Lee Patton. The age-old Grand Canyon becomes more and more ominous as a group of volunteers fight to survive alone in nature and uncover a murderer among them. (978-1-63679-047-3)

Highland Whirl by Anna Larner. Opposites attract in the Scottish Highlands, when feisty Alice Campbell falls for city-girl-about-town Roxanne Barns. (978-1-63555-892-0)

Humbug by Amanda Radley. With the corporate Christmas party in jeopardy, CEO Rosalind Caldwell hires Christmas Girl Ellie Pearce as her personal assistant. The only problem is, Ellie isn't a PA, has never planned a party, and develops a ridiculous crush on her totally intimidating new boss. (978-1-63555-965-1)

On the Rocks by Georgia Beers. Schoolteacher Vanessa Martini makes no apologies for her dating checklist, and newly single mom Grace Chapman ticks all Vanessa's Do Not Date boxes. Of course, they're never going to fall in love. (978-1-63555-989-7)

Song of Serenity by Brey Willows. Arguing with the Muse of music and justice is complicated, falling in love with her even more so. (978-1-63679-015-2)

The Christmas Proposal by Lisa Moreau. Stranded together in a Christmas village on a snowy mountain, Grace and Bridget face their past and question their dreams for the future. (978-1-63555-648-3)

The Infinite Summer by Morgan Lee Miller. While spending the summer with her dad in a small beach town, Remi Brenner falls for Harper Hebert and accidentally finds herself tangled up in an intense restaurant rivalry between her famous stepmom and her first love. (978-1-63555-969-9)

Wisdom by Jesse J. Thoma. When Sophia and Reggie are chosen for the governor's new community design team and tasked with tackling substance abuse and mental health issues, battle lines are drawn even as sparks fly. (978-1-63555-886-9)

A Convenient Arrangement by Aurora Rey and Jaime Clevenger. Cuffing season has come for lesbians, and for Jess Archer and Cody Dawson, their convenient arrangement becomes anything but. (978-1-63555-818-0)

An Alaskan Wedding by Nance Sparks. The last thing either Andrea or Riley expects is to bump into the one who broke her heart fifteen years ago, but when they meet at the welcome party, their feelings come rushing back. (978-1-63679-053-4)

Beulah Lodge by Cathy Dunnell. It's 1874, and newly engaged Ruth Mallowes is set on marriage and life as a missionary... until she falls in love with the housemaid at Beulah Lodge. (978-1-63679-007-7)

Gia's Gems by Toni Logan. When Lindsey Speyer discovers that popular travel columnist Gia Williams is a complete fake and threatens to expose her, blackmail has never been so sexy. (978-1-63555-917-0)

Holiday Wishes & Mistletoe Kisses by M. Ullrich. Four holidays, four couples, four chances to make their wishes come true. (978-1-63555-760-2)

Love By Proxy by Dena Blake. Tess has a secret crush on her best friend, Sophie, so the last thing she wants is to help Sophie fall in love with someone else, but how can she stand in the way of her happiness? (978-1-63555-973-6)

Loyalty, Love, & Vermouth by Eric Peterson. A comic valentine to a gay man's family of choice, including the ones with cold noses and four paws. (978-1-63555-997-2)

Marry Me by Melissa Brayden. Allison Hale attempts to plan the wedding of the century to a man who could save her family's business, if only she wasn't falling for her wedding planner, Megan Kinkaid. (978-1-63555-932-3)

Pathway to Love by Radclyffe. Courtney Valentine is looking for a woman exactly like Ben—smart, sexy, and not in the market for anything serious. All she has to do is convince Ben that sex-without-strings is the perfect pathway to pleasure. (978-1-63679-110-4)

Sweet Surprise by Jenny Frame. Flora and Mac never thought they'd ever see each other again, but when Mac opens up her barber shop right next to Flora's sweet shop, their connection comes roaring back. (978-1-63679-001-5)

The Edge of Yesterday by CJ Birch. Easton Gray is sent from the future to save humanity from technological disaster. When she's forced to target the woman she's falling in love with, can Easton do what's needed to save humanity? (978-1-63679-025-1)

The Scout and the Scoundrel by Barbara Ann Wright. With unexpected danger surrounding them, Zara and Roni are stuck between duty and survival, with little room for exploring their feelings, especially love. (978-1-63555-978-1)

Bury Me in Shadows by Greg Herren. College student Jake Chapman is forced to spend the summer at his dying grandmother's home and soon finds danger from long-buried family secrets. (978-1-63555-993-4)

Can't Leave Love by Kimberly Cooper Griffin. Sophia and Pru have no intention of falling in love, but sometimes love happens when and where you least expect it. (978-1-636790041-1)

Free Fall at Angel Creek by Julie Tizard. Detective Dee Rawlings and aircraft accident investigator Dr. River Dawson use conflicting methods to find answers when a plane goes missing, while overcoming surprising threats, and discovering an unlikely chance at love. (978-1-63555-884-5)

Love's Compromise by Cass Sellars. For Piper Holthaus and Brook Myers, will professional dreams and past baggage stop two hearts from realizing they are meant for each other? (978-1-63555-942-2)

Not All a Dream by Sophia Kell Hagin. Hester has lost the woman she loved and the world has descended into relentless dark and cold. But giving up will have to wait when she stumbles upon people who help her survive. (978-1-63679-067-1)

Protecting the Lady by Amanda Radley. If Eve Webb had known she'd be protecting royalty, she'd never have taken the job as bodyguard, but as the threat to Lady Katherine's life draws closer, she'll do whatever it takes to save her, and may just lose her heart in the process. (978-1-63679-003-9)

The Secrets of Willowra by Kadyan. A family saga of three women, their homestead called Willowra in the Australian outback, and the secrets that link them all. (978-1-63679-064-0)

Trial by Fire by Carsen Taite. When prosecutor Lennox Roy and public defender Wren Bishop become fierce adversaries in a headline-grabbing arson case, their attraction ignites a passion that leads them both to question their assumptions about the law, the truth, and each other. (978-1-63555-860-9)

Turbulent Waves by Ali Vali. Kai Merlin and Vivien Palmer plan their future together as hostile forces make their own plans to destroy what they have, as well as all those they love. (978-1-63679-011-4)

Unbreakable by Cari Hunter. When Dr. Grace Kendal is forced at gunpoint to help an injured woman, she is dragged into a nightmare where nothing is quite as it seems, and their lives aren't the only ones on the line. (978-1-63555-961-3)

Veterinary Surgeon by Nancy Wheelton. When dangerous drugs are stolen from the veterinary clinic, Mitch investigates and Kay becomes a suspect. As pride and professions clash, love seems impossible. (978-1-63679-043-5)